The Discarded Daughter
Book 4 – Loving & Living

A Pride & Prejudice Variation
By Shana Granderson, A Lady

CONTENTS

DEDICATION

This book, like all that I write, is dedicated to the love of life, the holder of my heart. You are my one and only and you complete me. You make it all worthwhile and my world revolves around you.

ACKNOWLEDGEMENT & THANK YOU

First and foremost, thank you E.C.S. for standing by me while I dedicate many hours to my craft. You are my shining light and my one and only.

I want to thank my Alpha, Will Jamison and my Betas Caroline Piediscalzi Lippert, and Kimbelle Pease. A special thank you to Kimbelle who had been a great help and has dedicated much time and effort to making this book better. To both Gayle Surrette and Carol for taking on the role of proof-reader and final editing, a huge thank you to you. All of you who have assisted me please know that your assistance is most appreciated.

Thank you to Veronica Martinez Medellin who created the cover art.

My undying love and appreciation to Jane Austen for her incredible literary masterpieces is more than can be expressed adequately here. I also thank all of the JAFF readers who make writing these stories a pleasure.

INTRODUCTION

This is the final book in a 4-book series.

At the end of Book 3, Mrs. Fitzpatrick AKA Mrs. Catherine de Bourgh (her title having been stripped), unleashed her final revenge. Her pet Wickham plans to finish the job of killing Lady Elizabeth and then he wants to abscond with Georgiana Darcy. The book opens with the results of the ambush and its direct aftermath. The plant, Jones, tries to bargain for his freedom, we see if he had anything of value to trade.

What happens to the conspirators and do they all reap their just rewards? Are any of the heroes harmed? All of these questions are answered in the first few chapters of Book 4.

The final book in the series follows the lives of the main characters as they love, live, and move forward. Another potential villain raises his ugly head, and we see who steps in to protect Lady Elizabeth this time.

William Darcy is finally able to stop crossing out dates on his calendar when Lady Elizabeth comes into society and has her ball. We follow the couple that we all love so very much from betrothal to marriage and into the future. At the same time, we get a glimpse of the lives of some of the characters that have been around Lady Elizabeth from the beginning of this series.

Near the end of the book, we find out about a most unexpected pairing. That dear reader will be the subject of a future sequel to the Discarded Daughter series. I thank you for reading my stories.

CHAPTER 1

Later the day of the attack:

Mrs. Fitzpatrick, or more correctly Mrs. de Bourgh, was in shock. All her dreams of revenge and dominance had been washed away like debris in a dry riverbed after a heavy rain. She did not want to believe it, but her current situation and the men of her former family all glaring at her gave a lie to her wish.

When everything went wrong, the former *Lady* Catherine de Bourgh could not fathom what was happening; she could not understand how this could result from her meticulous planning. How could a plan she devised and deemed to be perfect become such a disaster? She, a great lady, was bound like a common criminal, and a carriage was being made ready to transport her to gaol where, as she understood, *she* was to stand trial for the murder of some inconsequential maid that happened some years ago--well, and that of her late husband. And, apparently, they called the small matter of attempted murder of many people a crime. She had not actually been able to commit those crimes!

At some point in her ravings, Catherine de Bourgh had retorted to a comment about her killing her husband in a way that admitted she had, thus increasing her murder count from one to two. And now, no matter how much she screeched for them to end this farce, no one was paying heed. A point was reached when they had heard more than enough of her caterwauling, so one of the men gagged her, with both Richard's and Andrew's permission.

Why did people continuously refuse to follow her direction?

That was it! The failure was not in her plan but with the dim-wits who tried to execute it. They must have missed a critical step and look at the trouble it now caused her. She was sure, though, that as soon as she ordered the judge to set her free, he would do so. She ignored what her former brother-in-law had said about her secret spy not being so secret and that her family had planned her downfall, only giving her the illusion of being in control.

Not only had Pemberley slipped through her fingers again, but her house and all of her money were to be given to the family of a servant! Why should these lowlifes take what was rightfully hers just because she killed their daughter? She was a servant! It was her right to treat servants as she saw fit. They could not have paid her a greater insult if they had tried, given what her former brother-in-law and her late brother's whelps had decided to do with her money and property.

Catherine de Bourgh was now penniless, the same as the nobodies that she so disdained. The funds that she held in her carriage to pay the men were forfeit, and her erstwhile Darcy nephew had taken her private ledger that listed the banks and accounts, along with the names that she had used on each one.

Her former brother Darcy had told her that they would have a judge's order by morning ordering the banks to turn over all of her funds, and they would be disbursed to the family of the maid they claimed she had killed. It would be their choice to reside in the house in Packwood or sell it. If only she could escape.

No matter how deep her delusion, she was bound, gagged, and in irons, so no matter how much she desired to be free, she would never be again. Her destination was the Old Bailey in London, where she would answer for her crimes, and without a miracle from on high, she would swing. The fact that she still believed that she had the power to order things as she wished would not change the fate that awaited her in London.

In terrible shape after saying the wrong thing to the wrong person, Wickham was on his way to the gaol in Lambton. His sentence would be carried out in the morning, and he would be hung—if he survived the night. All of the hired criminals, including McLamb, minus the handful who had stupidly tried to resist, were under arrest. McLamb was fuming in the back of a wagon, cursing the day that he ever heard of Mrs. Fitzpatrick, or de Bourgh, or whatever her name was. The only question to be answered for McLamb and the rest of the men was would it be the noose or transportation without the option to return to England?

Earlier, as the attack began:

McLamb stood and pointed his pistol at the lead carriage's driver, proclaiming "Stand and deliver" while his men aimed their weapons at all five carriages; his triumphant smirk was wiped off his face in the next instant.

"All of you! Raise your hands NOW!" he heard from behind him. He had been so focused on his intended victims that he had not noticed the wall of men that had materialised, seemingly from nowhere, and surrounded them. If that was not bad enough, there were weapons pointed at them from the insides and tops of each carriage. McLamb saw that his men were outnumbered more than two to one. He was not about to give his life for the woman who had hired him. He was the first to lower his pistol, dropping it before raising his hands, telling his men to do the same. She was not worth any of his men dying for.

Mrs. Fitzpatrick was about to jump up and scream that they should kill all of them when her two footmen pulled their pistols from their belts. It was the last actions of their misspent lives. Before either could raise his weapon, they were cut down by a volley of shots. Three more of McLamb's men made the same mistake and quickly met the same end. After that, every mercenary dropped his weapons and raised his hands high.

As she sat in shock from the loud reports of the shots which were so close to her, and once the gun smoke cleared, she stared at the bodies of her men lying near her. Her shock increased tenfold when she heard the voice behind her.

"Did we spoil your plan, *Aunt*?" Andrew spat the last word out as if he had a bad taste in his mouth. "I thought that you were always right. so how is it that you have finally been captured, and your men are now dead or captured?"

"How dare you!" she demanded hotly.

"How dare we what, Mrs. de Bourgh?" George asked from behind her. "How dare we know all about Jones? How dare we send you notes in his stead? How dare we foil your plans to commit mass murder of men, women, and *children*? Or how dare we stand up to an insane murderer like yourself?"

"I should have poisoned all of you the same as I did that useless Louis de Bourgh," she spat back.

"Thank you for admitting to a second murder, Mrs. de Bourgh. Unfortunately, they will not be able to hang you more than once," her former brother told her with no feeling for the woman that sat spluttering before him. She started to scream and screech her vitriol, and after a minute or two, Andrew nodded to one of their men to gag the woman, and none too gently.

~~~~~~~/~~~~~~~

As they were dealing with the delusional *mastermind*, Will was searching her carriage. It seemed the driver had run off, and the carriage was unguarded; however, the guards with Will were vigilant and would take no chances. Will found nothing of consequence until he spied the corner of an oilskin pouch sticking out from under a seat. In it, he discovered the deed to her house in Packwood, account statements from the three banks among which she had divided her money, and all of her account books showing the name of each alias that she had used. The books were just as poorly kept as those at Rosings used to be when under her tenure. Before he headed back toward his father, he put everything back in the pouch to hand to him, knowing that his father would want to see all that he had discovered.

~~~~~~~/~~~~~~~

George Wickham could not comprehend what was happening. It seemed that not only would he not get to kill the foundling and spirit, Miss Darcy, to Gretna Green and marry her, but he had just seen an up-close demonstration proving that the men with weapons trained on him and the old bat's surviving men would not hesitate to shoot him if he made a wrong move.

Being the coward he was, he decided that his only slightly viable option was to slip away in all of the confusion as he was a yard or two away from the rest of the men. He had hoped that he had not been noticed as no one had turned in his direction. While he was contemplating how to make his getaway, he had not heard the stealthy approach of some men as they closed in. He suddenly sensed that there was a presence behind him, and he turned slowly with his hands raised, not wanting to give the man an excuse to shoot him.

Wickham did not make it all the way around to face them before a fist connected with his face, which seemed to have the force of a horse kicking him with all its strength. The blow knocked him back into a tree. At first, he was too dazed to see who his assailant was. As his vision cleared, he saw a seething Richard Fitzwilliam in regimentals standing in front of him, his fists still balled and ready.

"Did you think I would allow you the easy way out at the end of the hangman's noose only, did you, Wickham?" As he spoke, Richard unsheathed his sabre, ready to use it if needed.

Wickham made the mistake of opening his mouth to try to taunt Richard as he used to when they were both lads at Pemberley. "It is a pity my aim was not better, so I could have put that mongrel foundling…" Whatever he was about to say was lost in his scream of pain as Richard had dropped his sabre and started to pummel Wickham with blows, each one harder than the one before.

There was a sickening sound when Whickham's nose broke, sending blood spraying in all directions. Most of his teeth were dislodged from his mouth, and the force of the last blow drove him back into the tree behind him. His arm snapped when he slammed into the tree with his arm in an awkward position. Wickham, having soiled himself, was lying moaning in a semi-consciousness heap on the forest floor.

Andrew and Will had come over to stand next to Richard, and

had he not done such a good job on the blackguard already, they would have happily added their own blows to those Richard had doled out.

Right on cue, the constable and two of his men arrived from Lambton, putting what was left of Wickham in a cart. By morning, his worthless life would be over, one way or the other.

The four men with Perry, who had been toward the rear of the entourage, walked to where Mrs. de Bourgh was trussed up and gagged. George pulled her oilskin pouch from his satchel, which caused her eyes to grow wide; there were muffled sounds as she tried to yell.

"Thank you for all of the information about your names and bank accounts. After we receive an order for the release of your funds from a judge, all of the funds and property will be turned over to the family of the maid that you murdered!" Mrs. de Bourgh tried to jump up, but before she could stand, two men dragged her toward the old and uncomfortable carriage which would convey her to London.

McLamb and his surviving men, still under heavy guard, were rounded up, clapped in irons, and unceremoniously placed in carts. As the Lambton gaol could not accommodate them all, they would join Jones in the coal cellar at Pemberley. Once the men had time to relax and meet with the local magistrate, their fates would be decided.

~~~~~~~/~~~~~~~

Branch had not seen a plan executed so flawlessly in his fifteen years in the King's Army. He supposed that it helped that the men who opposed them did not seem to be the best or brightest the realm had to offer. Even with this over, he was not worried about the future. True, this threat had been eliminated, but the master and his nephew, the Earl, had promised that none of the men who worked as guards and outriders would be let go. Those who did not receive positions at either of the two estates would be placed at one of the satellite estates or at one of the houses in Town if they so desired. A high percentage of guards and outriders would be retained in their current positions.

~~~~~~~/~~~~~~~

Before he ran afoul of his wife and the party waiting for news, Andrew dispatched a rider to Pemberley to inform Bennet, Ashby, and the rest of the family that everything had gone according to plan and none of them or their men had come close to being injured. A postscript was added for his little sister, informing her that Wickham was captured, that the sentence would be carried out in the morning, and that the blackguard would never be able to hurt her or anyone else ever again.

~~~~~~~/~~~~~~~

When Douglas handed the note to Bennet, everyone held their collective breaths until they saw a wide smile spread across his face. "All of our loved ones and their men are safe—not even a scratch on any of them," he reported above the sounds of relief from all in the room. "Read the postscript from Andrew to you, Lizzy," Bennet told her as he handed her the note.

"Good!" she exclaimed, "That is no less than that miscreant deserves." Seeing the questioning look on her mother's face, she explained. "Wickham was captured, and he will never be free again."

"I pray that our brother was able to have his little chat with the blackguard," Marie enthused.

"We will hear all about it when our conquering heroes return," Lady Anne teased.

"It is such good news that Will, eh; hm, everyone is safe and uninjured." As Elizabeth tried to cover her slip of the tongue, she received a lot of knowing looks from members of their party.

Before the note arrived, Anne Ashby did not feel any remorse that her mother would soon be captured if she had not been already and would have to answer for her crimes. As the woman had never been a mother to her, there was no bond that she mourned the loss of. She had a wonderful mother and had two loving fathers. Ian hugged her in tightly to assure himself that his wife was well.

"All is as it should be Ian. As long as I have you and my family around me, I will never want anything. At least after she is cap-

SHANA GRANDERSON A LADY

tured, her days of hurting people will be over," Anne informed her husband as she rested her head on his chest.

"Do you think that this is the last of those that will try and hurt us?" Elizabeth asked Father Bennet as they resumed their chess game, which Bennet could see he had already lost.

"There will always be those in the world driven by greed or envy," Bennet replied. "That being said, I believe that after these miscreants are dealt with, there will not be more of their ilk trying and harm any members of our families. At least that is my hope."

"Mayhap that awful Miss Price will slink back into Town so you can set her down again," Georgiana said with a smile.

"I heard that her parents would not bring her back to Town. In fact, Aunt Maddie told me that they might be moving to the Americas as her father has suddenly found better opportunities there, added Jane."

"When will we be in London again?" Elizabeth asked her mother and sister-in-law Marie who were seated together.

"For the little season, I believe, Lizzy. Reggie will be one, and Andrew and I are looking forward to visiting London; it will be more than two years since we have been seen in London," Marie answered.

"When will the men return?" James asked.

"In a few hours, I hope," Lady Anne stated. Her niece had stopped seeing Catherine de Bourgh as her mother, and Anne Darcy no longer considered Catherine as her sister after she so callously murdered the maid at Rosings. How could she feel anything but disdain for one who planned to murder them all if her husband's supposition was correct?

~~~~~~~~/~~~~~~~~

The five family members rode back to Pemberley behind the carts carrying the prisoners. The carts with the criminals were well guarded by more than double the number of men that were in irons in the carts. A few had accompanied the constable back to Lambton with the bloody mess that was George Wickham in the bed of the cart. He was not in any physical shape to make an escape attempt, but that did not mean that their vigilance would relax. Men were known to do many unexpected or impossible things to escape death.

Mrs. de Bourgh was fuming in silence within the uncomfortable carriage in which she had been placed. Not being able to talk was a heavy punishment for her as there were so many commands that she needed to issue to the driver and the eight men guarding her. Six were riding, three on either side, one sat in the interior with her, and the last stood in the footman's position at the vehicle's rear.

The man sitting and watching her from his position on the forward-facing bench was very thankful that the lady would stay gagged. He was one of the men that had put the woman's ill-advised footmen down and had heard the invectives and stream of nonsense that emanated from her mouth. He shook his head at the antics of the woman, who seemed to be the only one not aware of her impending fate.

~~~~~~~/~~~~~~~

George Wickham could not have imagined more pain than what he was experiencing as the cart bumped along, taking him to his ultimate fate. He was conscious for the moment, but, thankfully for him, it was not long before he lost consciousness again. All of the bad choices that he made in his life flashed before his eyes.

It was too late, but he finally saw the folly in believing his mother and following her pronouncements like Gospel. She was a servant that envied anyone who had more than she did, and she had moulded him into her own likeness. If only he had woken up to the truth before he pulled the trigger killing his adoptive father. As he slipped back into blackness, he finally accepted that he had been the author of his own doom.

~~~~~~~/~~~~~~~

Jones was afraid, more afraid than he had ever been in his life. A few hours before, he had tried to trade information, only to be rebuffed.

When the big footman had come to drop off some bread and

water for him, he had played the one card he believed would extract him from this mess. "Afore ya' leave. I 'ave information on the one that 'ired me and sent me 'ere," he told the big man. "If I's allowed to go free, I's will tell all!"

"We don' need you!" Biggs spat back. "Right now, your employer an' all o' yer men 're bin captured. You 'ave nothin' that we need!"

Jones hung his head; then he remembered Branch. "What if I tell ya the name o' the man that 'elped me?" He was grasping at straws.

"You must be deaf!" Biggs snickered at the surprised man. "When you was captured, you was told that Branch was workin' for the master of Pemberley the whole time; 'e never 'elped you! 'e was writin' the notes that were sent, so we know all."

It was at that point that Jones realised that there was no escaping his fate. The only remaining question was if he would swing or be transported.

CHAPTER 2

A s the carts pulled up to the door that led down to the coal cellar, five men walked back from stables knowing that their planning and forethought had prevented a potential disaster for their family. They entered through the kitchen entrance, where Mrs. Reynold stuck her head out of her office.

"Master, you are not going to change before you see the family in the green drawing room, are you?" she inquired.

"We are not very clean and smell of horse," the master returned.

"I would suggest that all of you go to the drawing room first and let your family see you before you bathe and change. There will be hot water delivered for all five of you in twenty minutes," she promised.

As much as he wanted nothing more than a good soak in his bath, George Darcy recognised the wisdom in his long-time housekeeper's words. He nodded to Mrs. Reynolds, and he and the four others headed for the drawing room.

"George, William!" Lady Anne exclaimed as she saw her men enter. They were dirty and not very fresh smelling, but all she cared about was the visual proof that both of them and the other three were well.

"Itch!" Seventeen-year-old Elizabeth launched herself into her brother's arms after reassuring herself that Will was also not hurt. At the same time, Andrew and Perry were enfolded in their wives' arms.

"What happened to your hands, brother?" Elizabeth asked as she stepped back and lifted both his hands on which the knuckles were still bloody.

"We all need to go and bathe and change, and then we will tell all," George interrupted in a raised voice to stop the torrent of questions before they started.

"If Itch is anything to go by, then you all need a good hard scrub," Elizabeth teased as she held her nose, mocking her brother about his ripe odour.

"She has your sardonic wit, Thomas," Tammy said quietly to her husband, who nodded his agreement.

~~~~~~~/~~~~~~~

Once McLamb and the other men adjusted to the dim light of their temporary home, they saw a man was already being held in the cellar. The woman had told McLamb with pride about her secret spy at the estate and how her victims had no idea of his presence. From the spectacular failure of their plans, it seemed the spy was not a secret to the estate's inhabitants after all.

Once the guards checked that each man's irons were secure, the heavy metal door was locked. McLamb cornered the man that was there before them. "Did you tell 'em what we were about?" he asked menacingly. If he felt the man had betrayed them, he would not see another sunrise.

"No, one of 'em guards were workin' as an under-driver, and 'h was stealin' me messages an' writin' 'is own. I 'as no idea 'ow he knew, but I never tol' no one!" Jones told the man. Jones did not know who the man was but guessed correctly that he was the leader of the rest of the prisoners.

"'Ow come you 'ad no idea 'e was onto you?" McLamb asked. The glare in his eyes warned Jones not to lie.

"They let me alone until t'is mornin', jus' after the coaches left, they clapped me in irons and throwed me in 'ere," Jones rushed to explain.

"'Ave you 'eard what they will do wif us?" McLamb asked.

"Nothin'," Jones answered, "I be Jones."

"McLamb," came the reply. McLamb knew that over forty guards had accompanied them back from the site of the botched ambush, and there were very likely more at the estate. Since they were all in irons and in a windowless room with a heavy metal door, McLamb knew they had no chance of escape; their only hope was for transportation rather than a date with the hangman's noose.

~~~~~~~/~~~~~~~

By the time a broken and battered George Wickham was hauled into the gaol at Lambton, he was barely alive. The younger Mr. Harrison was summoned to examine the prisoner. He felt no sympathy for the wounded man as he knew what he had done before escaping all those years ago. His father had treated Lady Elizabeth alongside Mr. Finch, and he knew how badly injured she was because of the actions taken by the pathetic wretch moaning on the cot.

When he was done, he expressed the opinion that he doubted that the man would be alive to keep his appointment with the gallows come morning. In his examination, he had found three broken ribs. When he was informed that the man had angered one of the Fitzwilliam brothers who had punished him with his fists, he understood how his ribs could be broken, especially when he heard that one blow had caused his body to strike a tree trunk with great force. Considering that he was still breathing, the Fitzwilliam brother had exercised much restraint. Ben Harrison was sure that had a man hurt his sister like this one had Fitzwilliam's sister that he would have finished the job and felt no remorse once it was done.

He could see the bruising on the abdomen that was increasing, indicating internal injuries. He told the constable that the only thing to be done was to summon the pastor to give him last rites. Not only would he not survive the night, but the doctor also doubted that he would survive the hour. The vicar was sent for, but before he arrived, George Wickham breathed his last breath, finding some measure of peace at last.

~~~~~~~/~~~~~~~

Catherine de Bourgh was in high dudgeon and could not believe the degradation that she was suffering. The carriage conveying her to London had made a stop in Lambton where a maid joined them. Her bonds had not been loosened, nor had the gag been removed. When they stopped to rest at some dingy inn that as Lady Catherine de Bourgh, she would not have been caught dead in, the maid took her to the necessary and was helping her, as even then she was bound and gagged.

When they stopped to eat and drink, she was warned that if she said one word when the gag was removed to feed her, it would be replaced without delay. As soon as it was removed, she started to yell and vent her spleen, then, as she had been warned, it was replaced within seconds. To the vituperative woman, it was a heavy punishment indeed to have to hold her peace. An hour later, she was warned again. This time she remained silent long enough to drink some water and then was about to start screeching again but was pre-empted when the gag was put back in place. She was not a happy woman but still thought, as she always did, that she was a victim and was always right.

~~~~~~~/~~~~~~~

By the time the men returned downstairs after bathing and changing, it was only a few minutes before Douglas announced the meal, as no one had a proper meal earlier as they waited anxiously to hear what had happened. Much as she disliked her curiosity not being satisfied, a sentiment shared by almost all who had not been at the confrontation, Elizabeth told herself that she could wait until after dinner was over.

Elizabeth was next to Will, so he was able to offer his arm with much pleasure, and they entered the large dining parlour together. William pulled out a chair for Elizabeth next to Andrew and across from Jane and Perry. He took the seat on her other side before Richard, or his sister claimed it.

Richard saw that Will had seen through his intention to claim the seat next to Lizzy, so, with a big grin on his face, he went around the table and claimed a seat next to Jane while Georgiana sat next to her brother.

"Will, you not tell us anything, brother?" Georgiana asked plaintively.

"There will be no discussion on that subject at the table," said George Darcy.

Georgiana was but three seats away from her father when he issued his instruction with a mild rebuke before Will could formulate a reply. "After dinner, there will be no separation, and you will hear all and be able to ask your questions."

With a slight pout, Georgiana dropped the subject, not willing to gainsay her father. Thankfully the rest of dinner passed quickly, and all were soon heading for the drawing room.

The story was told from the moment that the leader of the libertines yelled out "stand and deliver" until the men returned home. As the tale was coming to an end, Douglas knocked, holding a silver salver; the master beckoned him over. The note was from young Mr. Harrison, who had attended the prisoner at the Lambton gaol.

"George Wickham succumbed to his injuries sustained during the botched attack today," the master of Pemberley announced with no emotion.

"It is normally sad when someone dies but not in this case! I am not sorry that he is gone and will never be able to hurt another," Elizabeth stated. Everyone agreed with her.

"According to the doctor, he broke some ribs when he hit a tree, and there was nothing to be done about the internal bleeding. In the end, he did not swing, but he did pay the price he owed for murder and attempted murder," Andrew stated after he took the note that his uncle offered him. "Our former aunt will join him soon."

"I am guessing that my sister did not enjoy being bound and gagged," Lady Anne stated. "It is my estimation that she does not realise the severity of her situation and thinks that with the force of her will, she will be able to extricate herself from these troubles."

"It is hard to believe how some of the men threw their lives away trying to go for their weapons. Did they not see the overwhelming odds arrayed against them?" Ian Ashby asked.

"Part of it was that I think they felt they had nothing to lose; it is also possible that they were confused. Either way, they paid with their lives," Richard surmised.

"It has been so many years that I hardly remember her as my mother," Anne stated. "She admitted to murdering my father?" she asked. The three men that had been present when she made her admission nodded. "Then she deserves whatever the price she has to pay. I am very happy all of her property and funds will go to the family of that poor maid she murdered; I want nothing from that woman!"

"What about the captives in the cellar?" Elizabeth asked.

"I would think transportation without the possibility of return for them," Andrew suggested. "Any of them who tried to fight back are no more, and I believe they did not fully know what was being asked of them."

"Except for the leader. McLamb, I believe is the name," Perry added. "As she had shared all with him, and he was more than willing to carry out her murderous plan, he should be tried, and if found guilty, strung up." There was no doubt in the room that the men would have carried out the orders, at least most of them would have if it had come to that. However, as Richard pointed out, from his military experience, you cannot always blame a soldier for his commander's orders.

Thus, it was decided that other than the leader of the group of men, they would suggest transportation. Those to be transported would be taken by cart to the nearest port with ships departing for the chosen shores. Perry and Andrew would use their combined influence to have an order of their permanent removal from England issued.

McLamb would be transferred to the Lambton gaol. There he would await trial to be held when the circuit judge made his rounds of the area in a fortnight.

After the recitation and all the questions were asked and answered, the family was able to truly relax for the first time since Jones's spying had become known. It seemed that all the guilty parties were dead or quite secure in their captivity.

~~~~~~~/~~~~~~~

The next morning, the door to the cellar opened, and the huge footman was joined by a second man no smaller than himself and four others. They roughly picked up a bewildered McLamb and exited the dank room, locking the door securely behind them.

McLamb hoped that he was to be interrogated again; however, that was not the case. He was taken into custody by Lambton's constable, who was accompanied by his two men. For extra security, four of Pemberley's outriders escorted the cart McLamb was thrown into.

After the five-mile journey to the town, McLamb finally realised that his fate was not to be transportation when he was dragged into the gaol cell, the same one in which Wickham had expired the night before. He tried to plead and beg, but no one was interested in his ravings—especially as all knew that he would have ordered the murder of the family that was the reason that the town thrived as it did.

A fortnight later, and after a trial of fewer than three hours, the circuit judge accepted the jury's unanimous verdict of guilty on all counts of attempted mass murder, and McLamb was sentenced to death to be carried out at dawn the following day. He spent his last day of life cursing the fact that he had ever met that insane woman from Packwood.

~~~~~~~/~~~~~~~

Less than a sennight after Andrew and Perry wrote to his Lordship, the chief judge at the Old Bailey, the transportation order was received. The men being held had been treated humanely once McLamb was extracted from their midst. Groups of eight would be taken outside for an hour or two each day, guarded by many well-armed men. They received two good meals each day, even some bread in-between, and they had been allowed to wash some of the stenches off by way of a dip in a pond.

The day of their departure from Pemberley, they were all brought out to the waiting carts, still in irons, and each group chained together. The Duke of Bedford read the order for them to be transported and explained that if any of them ever tried to return to England's shores that the sentence of death would be instituted.

Along with the other men, Jones knew that it could have been far worse, for they had heard the guards discussing McLamb's fate. At least they still had their lives—if they survived the three-month voyage to Australia.

~~~~~~~/~~~~~~~

After two of the most miserable days of her life, Catherine de Bourgh found herself ensconced in the woman's section of New-gate Prison. No matter how she cajoled, ordered, or commanded, she was ignored. On the day of her trial, she was taken to the Old Bailey. When she tried to claim that she should be addressed with the honorific 'Lady,' the judge pointed out that the title had long been stripped from her by order of the King. She continually yelled out in court, though his Lordship instructed her to be quiet. She ignored him, so after the fifth time, she was gagged and bound in the dock.

The former great lady had no barrister defending her due to her penniless state. Unfortunately, she had said nothing to help her case, especially when she admitted she was only sorry she had not succeeded in killing all of her former family.

There were witnesses from Rosings to the murder of the maid. They were followed by the Earl of Matlock, Mr. George Darcy, Lieutenant-Colonel Richard Fitzwilliam, Fitzwilliam Darcy, and Mr. Branch. They all testified to aspects of her attempted mass murder, as well as her confession to having poisoned her late husband. The defendant was never informed that on the same day of her trial, a judge had signed an order seizing all of Mrs. de Bourgh's bank accounts and property to be disbursed at the discretion of the Earl of Matlock.

As each of her outrages was enumerated, rotten fruit and vegetables were launched in her direction from the gallery until his Honour threated the next one to do so with an arrest. By the afternoon, the judge charged the jury to consider their verdict based on the presented facts.

An hour later, they returned a verdict of guilty as charged. The presiding judge prefaced the delivery of his judgement with a statement that as much as he hated to see a woman hang, in this case, there was no other option. He then read her sentence, and she was returned to Newgate for it to be carried out at dawn the following morning.

Her former family members declined to witness the hanging. Right up until the noose was placed around her neck, Catherine de Bourgh née Fitzwilliam was most displeased that things had not gone as she had commanded they should. It was in that instant before the trapdoor swung open that she considered that she might have been wrong.

~~~~~~~/~~~~~~~

John and Maude Cox had lived their whole lives in the village of Hunsford in a very modest dwelling with only two bedchambers, one for themselves and one for their remaining four children. Their oldest, Greta, had been murdered by the former mistress of Rosings Park before she fled. At least, the family had been receiving a monthly stipend from Rosings since the murder. It could not replace their Greta, who had just turned sixteen when she met her end, but the money did help the family survive.

About five days after the hanging of their daughter's murderer, they received the most unexpected visit from the master and mistress of Rosings. At first, they were embarrassed that such people would see how little they had, but they held their heads up high. Once they were seated with Anne and Ian accepting Mrs. Cox's proffer of tea so as not to insult her, Anne got to the reason for the call.

"I am sure you know that the woman who murdered both your daughter and my father is no more," she stated. Both husband and wife nodded. "When she was captured, it was discovered that she had a house on a few acres of land in Packwood, Warwickshire, and still had a substantial amount of funds left over hidden in various banks."

"Beggin' yer pardon misses, but why are yer tellin us this?" Mr. Cox ventured.

"My family and I made a decision. None of us want anything

from the woman. She took your daughter away from you; she was someone who could never be replaced. As restitution, all of that woman's remaining money and her property is yours to do with as you wish." Anne and Ian sat quietly as the couple opposite them seemed to sit in a stupor.

"A 'ouse and land?" Mr. Cox verified; certain he was dreaming.

"Yes, Mr. Cox; some farm animals, horses, and a carriage too. Also, there is a little more than five and twenty thousand pounds left of her money." Anne informed the two, who went silent again. To them, a hundred pounds would have been a Godsend, but the amount that was mentioned was inconceivable to them. Mrs. Cox promptly fainted.

After she was revived with salts that Anne had in her reticule, the lady of the house just sat and was shaking her head. "If we wan' ta stay in the area are we allowed, all our family be here," Mr. Cox finally managed.

Anne and Ian took as much time as the couple needed to explain that the house and any of the furnishings or animals in Packwood could be sold if that is what they preferred. In the end, they decided to do exactly that except for the horses which would be brought to them in Hunsford. Anne opined that the sum that the house and land would fetch would be enough for them to buy a small farm locally.

Anne told them to contact her when they were ready to buy a farm. She told them that she knew of a nice sized one that bordered her land with a house that would allow each child a bedchamber with a few to spare. She omitted the fact that it was her land, and she would sell it to them for whatever the house brought, which would be about half of the actual value of the one in Kent, but it would have the best of care, and that was a value of its own kind.

So it was that the family of the murdered maid became land-owning farmers. Finally, Catherine de Bourgh was of use to someone—even if it was in death.

CHAPTER 3

November/December 1798

The family was in Town for the little season. There were two among them who were happier than the rest that it had arrived. Will Darcy had less than three months to cross off his calendar; soon, he would be able to discard the one for 1798. The other who was as excited as he was and for similar reasons, although she was counting the days in her head, was Lady Elizabeth Rose Bennet Fitzwilliam.

When she was not in Will's company, he was the one that she was thinking of. She knew without any doubt that when he asked, whether it be courtship or a betrothal, her answer would be yes. She was sure that as soon as he was allowed to do so, he would ask one of the two questions, and despite hoping it was the latter option, she could not deny that so long as she knew he was hers, she would accept the former gratefully. And it would seem presumptuous but for their conversation within days after the last of the perpetrators of the attempted attack on the family had been dealt with.

Earlier that May at Pemberley

It was less than a sennight after the men had returned from the trial of Catherine de Bourgh. None had attended the hanging, but they had not left London before it occurred. Once the five men returned to Pemberley, it was within days that the Bennets and Rhys-Davies departed for their respective estates.

The night before the Ashbys' departure, the four siblings and Ian had sat together in a parlour discussing the events of the past months. Anne's brothers and sister wanted to make sure that she was well. All of them were grateful Ian had been there to support her as needed. Even though there had been no love for the condemned woman, she had been Anne's biological mother.

Anne had assured them, and in no uncertain terms, that the only thing that she felt sorrow about was the woman's victims. The judge had issued the order to seize all of the woman's assets. She and Ian were looking forward to meeting the murdered maid's family and presenting them with the recovered fortune and property deeds for the house the woman had unwittingly purchased for them.

As planned, the Ashbys departed the following day, and Richard went with them as he had to return to his unit. That left only the Darcys and Fitzwilliams at Pemberley. A few days later, Andrew, Marie, Will, Elizabeth, Georgiana, and Alex went for a long ride in Pemberley's fields with Aggie running alongside some of the time and others lying down and resting while watching her mistress and the usual complement of escorts.

At one point, maybe even intentionally, Will and Elizabeth were riding some twenty yards behind the other four. Will took the chance to ask a question that had been eating at him since the day he and the others had gone to finally end the threat to their family. "Lizzy, before we left, you said something that could be meant in more than one way," he opened somewhat nervously, knowing that he was intentionally skirting the limits of conversation that Andrew would permit, but some clarification was crucial; the conjectures were driving him mad at every turn of thought.

"Whatever can you mean, Will?" she responded playfully, "We had many conversations before you left, did we not?"

"You know, I mean the one we had during the ride we took the day before the confrontation," he returned.

"I do," Elizabeth blushed, agreeing that she knew *exactly* what he was referring to.

"I do not want to run afoul of Andrew, but am I correct in believing that you too were referring to the future as well as the present, the same as I was?" he asked, praying that her answer would be in the affirmative.

"You did not misunderstand my meaning, and, I am glad to say, it seems neither did I yours," she offered, her smile growing in time with his. Neither had said the words that were with each breath harder to hold in, but they finally knew that it was mutual in both regard and intent. Knowing it was now but a matter of time, both were able to face the coming months more easily, as they knew they would walk whatever path it was they would find together.

Back to November/December 1798

Since May, the family had known that something had transpired between the two, which caused the looks between them to become far more tender and contented than they had been before. The lack of anxiety, the lack of furtive glances, were more what gave them away than anything else. Will smiled to himself as he recalled the conversation he had had with Andrew before the Fitzwilliams had departed for Snowhaven.

Andrew had requested that Will join him in the sitting room of the suite he and Marie shared. Will had been asked to sit, but even before Andrew spoke, the look of concern l told Will what, or more correctly, who his cousin wanted to discuss.

"Have you declared yourself to my sister?" Andrew asked pointedly.

"That would be problematic as Anne is already married," Will replied, trying to inject some humour into the tense meeting.

"Do not be purposefully obtuse," Andrew shot back, "You know I mean Elizabeth!"

"Peace, Andrew, I was attempting humour, but I obviously have fewer skills than even I thought." Will held up a hand to ward off a retort, that statement gaining a slight smirk, and both settled into their seats.

"It is not the time to try though you will need it when facing Father Bennet. Now please, answer my question." Andrew nodded for him to speak.

"No, I have made no declaration. Do you think me devoid of all honour that I would do so knowing that it is against your expressed

wishes until after Lizzy is out?" He had not lied; he had made no declaration.

"So, you have no understanding with my sister?" Andrew pressed.

"If you are asking if we have a secret courtship or betrothal, then no, we do not. If she has me, I will be seeking such an understanding as soon as you allow me to pay my addresses to her." Will looked directly at his cousin so Andrew could read just how serious he was.

"I want her to have at least three months of a season, the same that I know father wanted for her, before you or anyone else declares for her," Andrew replied with resignation. "What will you ask her for?"

"Do you truly believe that we who have known one another for almost seventeen years would require a courtship to become well known to one another?" Will challenged.

Andrew was silent for a minute, and Will watched his cousin become reconciled to the fact that his baby sister would soon leave his home. "If Lizzy accepts you, I will grant whatever she does, but if it is a betrothal, it too will not be shorter than three months!"

They had shaken hands and parted.

Will could not but remember the conversation with pleasure. He knew what question he was going to ask but was determined to offer the option of courtship if Lizzy desired more time. After he had left Andrew's sitting room, Will had shared it with his parents.

Neither looked surprised, and both stated that they would love to have Lizzy as a daughter-in-law. The two younger Darcys were not canvassed, but there was no doubt that Georgiana had been hoping for years that Elizabeth would one day be her sister.

Andrew had relayed the contents of the conversation to both Marie, who was increasing again, and his mother. And just as it was when Will spoke to his parents, there was no surprise. The writing had been on the wall for a long, long time. For Elaine's part, it was true that she would miss Elizabeth not living in the same home, but with such an easy distance between their various homes, her baby would never be that far away.

~~~~~~~/~~~~~~~

Charles Bingley was the happiest of men as he was waiting at the front of St. Alfred's in Meryton; his friend Darcy was standing up for him. His niece Mary walked down the aisle, dropping rose petals, and then almost ran to sit next to her mother once her task was finished. Next, his soon-to-be sister-in-law Cara walked down the aisle to take her place opposite Darcy.

The vestibule doors opened, and Mr. Pierce indicated that the congregation should stand. Then she was walking toward him, Mandy Long, on her father's arm. He was about to marry the woman that he loved above all others.

He had delayed the wedding until they had passed the two-year marking of his father's death. Mrs. Bingley was out of mourning and, with Louisa and her mother, had planned a wedding breakfast that would be remembered in the area for a long time. Martha, wearing light colours for the first time in public, was sitting in the front pew on the side where her son was standing waiting for his bride. The Hursts, Martha Bingley, and the other family that had come from Yorkshire were with her and in the next two rows of pews.

Cheryl Long was sitting in the front pew across the aisle, waiting for her husband to join her after he handed Mandy over to her groom. The girls had come to be theirs because of tragedy, but their life had been much better because of their daughters. As Cara stood waiting for her sister to reach the altar, she was sure that their mama and papa were smiling on her from heaven as Mandy walked up the aisle on her father's arm.

Soon after, the new Mr. and Mrs. Charles Bingley were being announced by Nichols as they walked into the ballroom at Netherfield with all their family and friends clapping for them. Martha was no longer mistress of the estate Oscar had bought for her and his family, but she did not feel she was being pushed aside. Charles and Mandy had repeatedly stated that they would not hear of her moving to the small dower house and that she was wanted.

The Bennets, Rhys-Davies, Fitzwilliams, and Darcys had made the trip from Town to witness the wedding. It was at the wed-

SHANA GRANDERSON A LADY

ding breakfast that Franklin Lucas asked leave to introduce his fiancée, Miss Cassandra Howell, whose father had a small estate in neighbouring Essex. It was obvious that the two had a love match, and they received well wishes from all.

Two hours later, the new Mr. and Mrs. Bingley departed for Ramsgate, and those that had made the trip from London departed not long after to arrive at their various homes as dusk descended on the city.

~~~~~~~/~~~~~~~

A few days after their return to Town, Elizabeth, Georgiana, Amy, and Retta were on their way to Bond Street when the coachman had to pull the carriage up short due to an obstacle in the road. Two lads who thought that they had an easy, soft target advanced until Biggs and Johns stepped around from their place at the rear of the conveyance. The two stopped dead in their tracks, and then they noticed the four men on horseback, all pointing pistols at them.

"I tol' ya it were not a good idea," one said as he slapped his mate on the back of the head.

"'Ow wus I s'posed ta know about all them men," the second said as he rubbed the spot which was smarting.

"Why do you think that you can rob money from good people?" Elizabeth asked as she stood between her footmen, who were not happy that she had exited the carriage as they did not know if there was more danger lurking, so they were hypervigilant and signalled the outriders to take up station on either side of Lady Elizabeth.

"We 'ad no choice, mi'lady," the first one said.

"There is always a choice; you could work to earn money rather than try and steal it," Elizabeth said with her hands on her hips. The other three ladies decided to stay in the carriage with Mrs. Annesley.

"Our ma is sick an' we don 'ave money for medicine, mi'lady," the second lad said. "She needs it now, an' we need to work weeks ta earn enuf ta pay fir it, and in meanwhile our brother an' sister go 'ungry."

"Where does your mother live?" Elizabeth asked.

"Seven dials," the older-looking lad, who could not have been more than ten, answered.

"I will send two of the guards on horses, each of you can sit behind one of them. They will see if what you say is true, and if it be so, I will help you. But if you have lied, they will take you to the runners. Do you understand?" Elizabeth asked the lads. When both boys nodded, Elizabeth handed a ten-pound bank-note to one of the outriders with the instruction to verify the story. Each man lifted a boy up behind him.

Biggs suggested that a third rider accompany the other two, just in case. "If what you say is true, then one of our men will give you direction to come to my house on the morrow, and we will see what we can do for you. I hope for your sake what you told us was not a lie," Elizabeth stated before the guards urged their horses forward.

Johns quickly removed the obstacle with the minimum of effort, and they were soon underway again. "You were so brave to go outside and talk to those two, Lizzy," Georgiana stated with admiration.

"In hindsight, Gigi, I should not have exited the carriage until Biggs and Johns indicated that it was safe to do so; I was impetuous. Besides with Biggs and Johns, not to mention four outriders and the driver being armed, it was not so very brave, Gigi. They were but lads, and although I do not agree with the way that they were trying to help, if what they said is true, and I suspect that it is, then they were trying to save their mother and siblings," Elizabeth explained.

"What will you do if they come to Matlock House on the morrow?" Amy asked.

"That will depend on what the guards report back to me," Elizabeth replied.

"I would have never got out of the carriage either," Retta stated.

"Without all of the protection I had, neither would I," Elizabeth told her friend with a smile.

"In my opinion," Mrs. Annesley stated, having listened to the four up to now without interjecting, "What you did, as you pointed out to Miss Darcy, Lady Elizabeth, was impulsive and an unnecessary risk. You did not know if more men were hidden, so the correct course of action would have been to stay in the carriage with us," she told her charge, with mild rebuke.

"I acted without looking at all possibilities like I do when I play chess. Thank you for pointing that out to me, Mrs. Annesley," Elizabeth replied contritely.

The rest of the trip to modiste and then Gunter's was uneventful, and after dropping Amy and Retta off at their homes, the Matlock coach returned to Grosvenor Square.

~~~~~~~/~~~~~~~

When they arrived home, Elizabeth told Andrew all that had happened and made sure he knew that she was out of the door before her companion knew what she was about, leaving her with no choice but to stay with the three young ladies inside the vehicle.

Unsurprisingly, he agreed with Mrs. Annesley and chastised his sister for not thinking the situation through properly and getting her companion's permission before acting. Elizabeth apologised and promised never to do such a thing again. While they were talking, one of the guards who went with the lads was admitted to the study.

He confirmed that the boys had been honest about the situation but did not understand how sick their mother was, that she would not last too many more days. When asked, he informed the master and his sister that besides the two would-be thieves, there were five more children. The oldest lad was twelve and the youngest not yet two years old.

After Andrew dismissed the man with his thanks, Elizabeth turned to her brother. "Andrew, do you remember Mother Bennet telling us about the work that she and the committee do in Meryton and other places?"

"I do, Sprite. What idea have you in that pretty head of yours now?" he asked. He loved seeing his sister's compassionate nature at work.

"May I send a note to Mother Bennet to be here on the morrow, and rather than just the two boys, can we bring all seven children and their mother here so she can be comfortable at the end, at least?" she asked hopefully.

"There is no reason why not, Sprite," Andrew replied.

Elizabeth sat and dashed off a note to be carried three doors down by one of the footmen, then requested that her mother and Marie join herself and Andrew in the study.

Once the full story was told, both Elaine and Marie had the same visceral reaction as Andrew to Elizabeth's unwise decision but then were quickly in agreement with the plan to help the family. A note was received from Mother Bennet confirming that she would be there in the morning and that she would send a note to Jane and to Martha Bingley, who was with the Hursts at their London home.

When the rider returned with the news that they would all be moved out of the hovel that they had been trying to survive in, the two lads could not believe someone who could have just as easily turned them over to the runners was going to assist them; and their ma would see a real doctor!

The next morning, Mr. Tristan Bartholomew, the London physician of both the Darcys and Fitzwilliams, was waiting with the rest of the group when the two carts pulled into the mews at Matlock House. The mother was carried on a litter to a servant's room near the warmth of the kitchens, and the children were put in the three rooms next to where their mother was.

"With all of the funds that some very generous benefactor donated," Martha Bingley said as she looked at Jane, "taking these unfortunate children into the home that was built between Longbourn and Bennington Fields will be no problem. They will be raised in the county, be educated, and never want for food or clothing. The boys will learn trades if they have an inclination, and the girls will be prepared to go into good service positions. Best of all, they will all be kept together." Tammy nodded her agreement while Jane blushed at her gift, so publicly acknowledged.

"Why did we not think of it before, Marie! Can we talk to Aunts Anne and Rose, as well as you, Mama, and start a similar programme in Derbyshire?" Elizabeth asked excitedly.

"That is a capital idea, Lizzy," Marie replied as her hand went to her belly instinctively.

When Elizabeth's plan was put to Ladies Rose and Elaine, they agreed without reservation. With the help of Tammy Bennet and Martha Bingley, plans were drawn up to start instituting in Derbyshire the same programmes that the committee in Meryton had been running.

After the doctor examined the mother of the seven children, he informed them that she would be at peace in a few days. In his opinion, it was cancer, and there was nothing that would stop in the inevitable. The two oldest boys were summoned to the study, treated as the men they had attempted to be the day before, and as gently as possible, the truth of their mother's situation was explained to them.

There were tears shed as the boys worried about what would befall them and their five brothers and sisters. Tammy Bennet then laid out the plan which the adults had outlined to them for their approval on behalf of their family. The boys sat for a moment to the side of the study, and although incredibly sad about the impending death of their mother, we're relieved that all seven of them would be together and not in one of the dreaded workhouses. When asked about their father, they relayed that he had died of illness just after the youngest girl was born, which had begun the downfall to the straits in which they had been found.

Three days later, as Mr. Bartholomew predicted, the mother slipped from the mortal world and was finally at peace. The Fitzwilliams paid for a decent burial for her in one of the local church's graveyards. The two oldest boys had attended to watch as their mother was laid to rest. The next day, they were in carriages far finer than they ever imagined that they would ride in and on their way to Hertfordshire.

Until they arrived at the newly-built home where they would live, they had not grasped the truth of their situation, thinking that it could not be as the nice people had told them. From what the children could see, it was far better than anything that they imagined. The four older children, the two boys, and the two oldest girls were placed in bedchambers that each pair would share, and the youngest three were placed in the nursery.

Rather than ending up in gaol as they likely would have if they had attempted to rob anyone else, they were in the country, in a house with caring people, and were living a life with more luxury than they could have conjured in their wildest dreams. To them, Lady Elizabeth Fitzwilliam was the angel that had saved all their lives.

~~~~~~~/~~~~~~~

As plans for Christmas in Hertfordshire were finalised, the Derbyshire Committee, as they dubbed themselves, had grown to include Lady Anne Darcy as well. They were relishing the upcoming time that they would all be at Longbourn for Christmastide, wanting their plans finalised as soon as may be, and they would be able to pick the brains of all the ladies that ran the charitable foundation in Meryton.

Elizabeth felt a purpose like she had never before. She could have ended up in far worse straits than the seven children had been in if her brothers had not discovered her in Sherwood Forest. The shame she felt that she had not thought of emulating what was being done by Mother Bennet and her friends led to a determination that she would give back as much as she could. She was most pleased when she shared her vision with Will, and he was as committed as she was.

On the seventeenth day of December, all of the family members, including the Gardiners, left London for Longbourn and Christmastide in Hertfordshire. Elizabeth could not wait to see how the seven children were adjusting to their new situation.

CHAPTER 4

T he first thing that Elizabeth did the day after they arrived in Hertfordshire was to ride to the house where the seven children were staying. It was a short ride, and Elizabeth had the pleasure of Will and her Bennet siblings for company. Will rode next to her, as close as they could be without their mounts bumping into one another. Biggs, Johns, and several other guards rode near the party, as did two grooms.

When they reached the front of the house, now named *New Hope House*, they were met by the matron in charge. Elizabeth spied the four children, all clean and well-dressed, waiting impatiently for one of their caregivers to release them. The youngest, a little girl not yet two and very slight since the children had been given only one meal a day, was sucking her thumb and holding her oldest sister's hand tightly.

After a nod from one of the governesses employed at the home, the two boys took off like a shot out a cannon and ran to Elizabeth, hugging her tightly. "Now boys, we wait to be invited to hug someone; please allow Lady Elizabeth to breathe." the governess admonished but was unable to hide her smile.

"I am well," Elizabeth replied as she returned the hugs and then greeted each of the other children. The youngest one hid her head in her sister's skirts shyly. "I take it that you like your new home?"

"Yes, mi'lady, we do, ever so much," the oldest boy spoke for his younger brothers and sisters. "There is so much space 'ere!" he stated as he made a sweeping gesture toward the park and the treeline beyond it.

The children who were old enough to understand what happened to their mother mourned her as best they could. However, the sorrow of losing their mother was balanced with the vast material change in their situation. They would have thought that two meals a day were a luxury, but here they received three good meals a day with some snacks in-between. All of their needs were met, and the only downside for the boys was that they had to bathe every day; however, they could live with that disappointment for a full belly and the hope which they now had. All seven were happy to see Lady Elizabeth Fitzwilliam, who they saw as a guardian angel.

After visiting for an hour, the seven riders and their retinue returned to Longbourn. There would be a meeting that afternoon between all the ladies on the local foundation's committee and those who wanted to start an extension of the charity in Derbyshire and some of the other northern counties.

~~~~~~~/~~~~~~~

The meeting between the Derbyshire and Meryton committees was informative. "Do you think it would be effective if we acquire pledges from all of the landowners in our county?" Elizabeth asked.

"That is what we used to do, Lady Elizabeth, until her Grace gifted us with her gigantic donation. The money is invested with Gardiner and Associates, so we have more than enough from the dividends without having to expend a lot of time trying to raise funds," Mrs. Goulding shared.

"Mrs. Goulding, have I not asked you to address me as Jane as you always have when we are not in public?" Jane, who had now joined the Derbyshire committee, gave the lady a steady look.

"I apologise your...Jane, I will remember in future," Mrs. Goulding smiled at the young woman whose life had turned out as happy as she deserved. While the lady spoke to her sister, Elizabeth was deep in thought as she worked the puzzle in her mind, and then she had a plan. All she would need was Andrew to agree, and he very seldom denied her anything.

"Marie, Mama, did Father Bennet not add fifty thousand pounds to my dowry that already equalled that amount?" Elizabeth was never so vulgar as to discuss the size of her dowry, but on this day, she had a purpose and received the nods she expected. "That means that I have an obscene amount of money in my dowry. If I can convince my brother to allow it, I would like to seed our endeavours in Derbyshire and the surrounding area with half of my dowry."

"Are you sure, Lizzy?" Elaine asked, knowing full well that once her daughter made up her mind, there was no changing it, but in this, she could not imagine a better way to use the funds she and Will would never truly need.

"I am, Mama. I have a feeling that when and if I do marry," Elizabeth blushed at her mother's knowing arched brow, "that even if I only had ten thousand the same as Jane, never mind fifty thousand, I will not need it." Lady Anne beamed, she knew exactly who Elizabeth was referring to, and yes, the Darcy coffers were overflowing, so even with no dowry, it would not be an issue, for they would have gained a true treasure in her.

"It is your dowry, my beloved daughter, so if Andrew agrees, then it will be as you ask," Elaine said. The great pride in her daughter increased exponentially, and she too wondered why, after hearing about it for years, they were only starting this now.

"Snowhaven will add five and twenty thousand," Marie offered, knowing full well that it would not dent their finances and that her husband would agree, nay, insist.

"Pemberley will add the same," Lady Anne committed.

"And Longfield Meadows will match Lizzy's contribution," Jane added.

"With one hundred and fifty thousand pounds, that should bring in ten to fifteen thousand pounds per annum. I would say that the Derbyshire committee too, will not have any financial issues," Lady Lucas smiled, marvelling at the women she was in the company of.

While Elizabeth made notes, the ladies discussed the infrastructure and the types of staff that would be needed. Not only would the projects that they initiated be a Godsend for those in need, but it would be a boon to the local economies in employment, building, and once open, to the local shopkeepers.

"I think that we should follow the example that you have set here, and the first facilities should be near the towns of Matlock, Bedford, Lambton, and Kympton. We have more than enough funds so that once they are established, we will be able to look for additional sites for homes like New Hope House," Lady Anne suggested. Her suggestion was agreed to by both the ladies who would serve with her and their counterparts in Meryton.

"We will all work on the men to allot land for the houses when the time comes," Jane stated with a smile. There was no doubt that when asked, any of the men in question would happily grant the requests for land.

"As the seven Black children have no relatives, I would like to move them to Derbyshire—if they agree and desire to do so," Elizabeth stated, changing the subject. She felt a bond with the children because of what had happened to her when she was discarded. Yes, the situations were quite different, but there were similarities, and if not for the Fitzwilliams, her fate may have been as bad if not worse than these children would have faced.

"I would suggest that you allow them to settle in properly first. You remember why my husband did not try and demand that you come live with us at Longbourn, Lizzy?" Tammy asked gently.

"He did not want to cause the trauma of… I understand. They need to feel secure, and if I asked, they would agree to move to please me as they feel indebted to me." Elizabeth understood and refused to let her own desires be put ahead of the children's welfare.

"My recommendation is that you give them at least a year," Martha suggested. "By then, they will feel secure and know that this is not a temporary way station in their lives, but their new reality. If you still want them to consider Derbyshire, ask them then after you talk to their caregivers to ensure that the children are ready to hear that question."

"Do not forget that you will be able to see them whenever you visit your birth family, and I am sure that when you are in Town, with the easy distance and four and twenty miles of good road, you can be in the area as much as you desire," Cheryl Long added.

The meeting broke up, and soon after, Elizabeth sought her older brother. They met in his and Marie's sitting room. Once Andrew had been informed what Elizabeth was requesting to do with half of her dowry, he was silent for a while as he considered his sister's request.

"Are you sure this is what you desire, Sprite?" he asked, watching her excitement as she considered it with him.

"I am, Andrew," Elizabeth answered emphatically. "Even at half, my dowry is among the largest that any has. I have not seen it in our family, but there are many that I have observed that seem as if their whole aim in life is to accumulate more and more money, and they care not who they hurt in order to attain their goals.

"The average working-class person lives on what? Less than thirty pounds a year? I have started to ask myself when enough is enough! We give to charity as a family, but yet it is a fraction of a fraction of our earnings, never mind our financial worth. I want to enjoy life, and a big part of that enjoyment will be help- ing others who have a genuine need," Elizabeth was adamant. "I should do what Jane did and turn over all of my dowries to char- ity, but before you object, I will not…yet. I want to have funds so we can live, not live to increase our wealth. So yes, Andrew, I am sure that this is what I want to do."

"Then it will be so. As soon as the committee opens accounts for the charity, the funds will be transferred," Andrew promised.

"We are contributing five and twenty thousand pounds to the Derbyshire committee's funds, and I daresay that it will not be long before Lizzy finds the parcel of land that she will want do- nated to build the facilities in Derbyshire," Marie informed her husband. Before he could react to her statement, she exclaimed: "Ooh, I just felt it!"

"Is all well with our…" Andrew stopped himself as they had not made a public announcement yet.

"There is no need to be coy, big brother. If you think that any of us are not aware that my sister is with child, then you are deluding yourself. We have all seen the signs but would never approach either of you until you were ready to make it official," Elizabeth informed the couple with a huge smile on her face.

"Our child just moved!" Marie exclaimed.

"I will have to make an *announcement* at dinner," Andrew said as he grinned.

"Should I inform the family that they should all look surprised?" Elizabeth teased her brother and sister.

"Just you wait, Sprite!" Andrew rubbed his sister's head playfully. "I will get you back when you least expect it."

"When will Itch arrive?" Elizabeth asked; she was concerned that they had not seen much of Richard lately.

"He will arrive the morning of Christmas Eve. The generals have been getting nervous. There is a French general, a Corsican, who has risen through the ranks with very fast and was charismatic man. Napoleon Bonaparte is his name, I believe. The high command is concerned that he has higher aspirations than that of being a general, and his eye is cast beyond France's borders, which is very possible based on speeches and comments that have been attributed to him," Andrew explained.

"Please let us work on our brother to resign and sell his commission before there is a war," begged a worried Elizabeth. "He has Brookfield that earns a healthy income, so he does not need to be in the Army."

"It has never been a need for Richard, Sprite," Andrew reminded her gently. "He told Mother and Father once that he felt a calling. He would not resign to escape going to war, nor would I disrespect him by asking him to. He will leave and take up full management of Brookfield when he is ready and not a moment before."

"If anything happens to Itch, it will devastate me," Elizabeth stated the obvious. That would be true for the whole family if, heaven forbid, that event ever came to pass.

~~~~~~~/~~~~~~~

In his chambers, William Darcy was holding up his calendar

for 1798. He looked with satisfaction at the last sheet of parchment, which boldly pronounced 'December 1798' at the top of the page. He took his pencil and blacked out the first and twentieth day of December.

He then picked up and looked at the next calendar for 1799; there were three important dates circled in red ink. First was the ninth day of January—the day they would all return to London. Next, the sixteenth day was circled—the day that Lizzy officially joined the society and made her curtsy before the queen. Last, though, was the most important date of them all. Friday, the eighteenth day of January 1799—the day of Lizzy's coming out ball.

Will had approached Andrew a few days before and remembered the conversation vividly.

"You asked to see me, Will?" Andrew inquired.

"Yes, Andrew. I need to ask your permission to ask Lizzy something." As he suspected, Andrew jumped to the wrong conclusion if his face was anything to go by. Will saw the mounting storm clouds, so he continued quickly. "No, Andrew, not that question; I know and honour your restrictions." Will saw his cousin visibly relax. "I would like to request three dances from Lizzy. The second, supper, and final sets."

He watched as the emotions played across Andrew's face. "I was about to refuse you, but I remember how being in love with Marie before, I was allowed to declare myself," Andrew sighed. "You may request the sets, but after this ball, no more than two sets per ball until and unless she accepts a courtship or betrothal from you. Either I, Richard, or one of our other male relatives will open each ball with her that she attends. If she grants them, you are free to request the supper and final sets with her."

Will had been elated by the answer, thanked his older cousin profusely, and then set out to find the woman he loved. He found her sitting quietly in Longbourn's library with Miss Annesley across the room from her, out of earshot but able to see all.

"Lizzy, may I have a moment of your time?" he asked. She placed a bookmark, set the book on the table in front of her, and then looked

up at him expectantly. *"I would like to request some sets at your coming-out ball…"* She interjected before he completed his request.

"If they are the second, supper, and final as we discussed some months ago? I am mistaken as I had thought it was understood. As it seems you were in doubt, let me remind you that they are already reserved for you, Will," she replied with a blush at being so forward.

He had given her a dimple revealing smile, and had he been allowed, would have kissed her there and then; he could not wait until he could do that. "Thank you, Lizzy. I have Andrew's permission, for we previously agreed on three sets at your coming out, but no more than two after that until we have an understanding—if we have one in our future. *He was encouraged to see his cousin blush, nodding that she understood, then again picked up her book.*

As he stared at the calendar, he counted the days, only seven and twenty more days to the ball. Less than a month, which was but a small wait considering that he had started crossing days off almost two years ago.

<center>~~~~~~~/~~~~~~~</center>

Andrew made the announcement that surprised no one at dinner. That everyone suspected in no way diminished the level of well-wishes the couple received once it had been shared. After dinner, when the ladies were sitting in the music room, and Georgiana and Kitty entertained them with a duet, Jane beckoned Elizabeth to join her on a settee away from the body of the ladies.

"Promise me that what I am about to tell you will not pass your lips until I tell you that the news is public." Jane opened.

"You have my complete discretion, sister, on my honour," Elizabeth promised.

"You are the next to know after Perry, I missed my second month's courses, and we believe that I am with child," Jane revealed to her younger sister. Elizabeth enfolded her sister in her arms and hugged her at length.

"It means so much that you chose to share this news with me, after Perry," Elizabeth whispered in Jane's ear, hugging her tighter in appreciation.

"If you had grown up at Longbourn, I am sure that we would have shared confidences with one another all the time and would have been the best of friends for many years now, so naturally, you were the one to be told. Once I feel the quickening, I will tell my Mama and Mother Rose before Perry makes an announcement to the family. By then, my mother-in-law will be an old hand at being a grandmama, but I am so excited for Mama and Papa to be able to enjoy their first grandchild," Jane explained quietly.

"You are too good, Jane," Elizabeth stated.

"Until you make me angry," Jane warned with a smile.

"Lizzy, if you and Jane are finished conspiring, the courier brought a bag of post from Town today. There has not been a single 'no' to the invitation for your coming-out ball. Your dance card will be full as soon as the receiving line is over," her mother shared.

"It is already half full, Mama," Elizabeth owned.

"With whom?" Aunt Anne inquired, relatively sure that her son's name would be mentioned more than once.

"Andrew will dance the first dance of the opening set, Father Bennet the second dance, Will follows, then Itch, William, Uncle George is next. I have one open before supper and then Will for the supper set. Perry is the first after supper, followed by Ian, then the rest are open until the final set, which is reserved," she informed the ladies, hoping that no one would ask the identity of the partner for the final set. She had no such luck.

"Who is the lucky man to dance the last set with you, Lizzy?" Aunt Anne asked, fairly sure she knew the answer to her question.

"Your son," Lizzy admitted, uncharacteristically shy as she did. Georgiana, who was sitting next to her cousin and best friend, gasped.

"You are dancing three with Will!" she blurted out.

"I am," Lizzy's courage rose.

"There will be a roar of speculation, and it will be widely reported in the gossip rags," her mother pointed out.

"Let them talk!" came the defiant response. Before anyone could comment, the men re-joined the ladies.

"Did we miss something?" Will asked as he went to Lizzy, who had looked at him in a fit of pique. Try as he might, he could not fathom why his ladylove looked peeved while the rest of the ladies in the room were very much diverted.

CHAPTER 5

The coming-out ball would be held at Matlock House and hosted jointly by the Fitzwilliam and Bennet families. On the evening of the sixteenth of January, the day of Lizzy's curtsey, a formal dinner would be held at Bennet House for the family and some close friends. Elaine and Tammy, who were organising the ball jointly, had a cadre of assistants in the form of Jane, Lady Rose, Marie, both Annes, Maddie Gardiner, Hattie Phillips, Sarah de Melville, and Gillian Ashby.

Before they had left Town for the Christmastide break, all the plans for Elizabeth's coming-out ball were in place. As they were tangentially related through Jane and Perry, and because of the Queen's interest in Elizabeth over the years, an invitation to Elizabeth's ball was sent to Buckingham House.

The Queen's lady in waiting, the Duchess of Kent, had written a reply to the Dowager Countess Matlock that Prince Edward and Princess Elizabeth would represent the royal family. Once the Prince's attendance was known, a small adjustment had to be made to the first set. The Prince would lead Elizabeth onto the floor and dance the first few movements with her, then Andrew would take over and dance the rest of the first half of the set as originally planned.

Between making sure that everything was in order with the upcoming activities surrounding Elizabeth's launch into society and the plans for the Derbyshire Committee, there was not as much time for relaxation as there otherwise would have been for the ladies of the families.

~~~~~~~/~~~~~~~

On Sunday morning, the day before Christmas Eve, Elizabeth decided that she needed a long ramble before breaking her fast regardless of the cold. She dressed warmly, donning her sable lined gloves and heavy fur-lined coat. Although she would have preferred to sleep in front of the warm fire, Aggie dutifully followed her mistress, as did Biggs and Johns a little way behind them. Elizabeth remembered the vista that she had viewed from Oakham Mount and decided to head in that direction. As she walked with Aggie barking at the stray rabbit, she decried the fact that she had not had as much time with Will as she would have liked due to all that had needed to be accomplished of late.

Her mother and Mother Bennet had involved her in planning her ball as they had not wanted to make unilateral decisions, only to discover too late that they were not reflective of Elizabeth's preferences. As she came out of the trees at the path leading up the side of the hill that the locals named a 'Mount,' she was jolted out of her current mood and became excited when she spied Zeus on a long tether as he breakfasted on the available grass and shrubs.

When she crested the top, Aggie gave a warning growl, then recognised that it was Will and walked up to him, tail wagging and nudging his hand in a bid to get him to scratch behind her ears. As her two footmen had seen their mistress's cousin's horse, they had relaxed, knowing it was a family member and not a stranger on the crest.

"Good morning, Will," Elizabeth greeted her cousin as she approached the spot where he was sitting under the oak tree on the big rock. Aggie had already flopped down and was on her way to slumber.

"Morning, Lizzy," he returned, thanking his lucky stars that his gamble on her taking a ramble before church paid off.

"It is a cold morning, is it not?" she asked as she pulled her winter coat around her shoulders.

"Here, take my jacket; you are cold!" He stood, quickly unbuttoning the top button. She placed her hand on his arm, so he went still. It was not just her touch that stayed his actions; it was her proximity. He could smell her lavender scent even through the layers that she had on. She was so close all he had to do was bend his head, and their lips would meet. He dropped his head slightly, and her eyes fluttered closed in anticipation. He would perhaps have broken a promise were it not for the loud cough behind them. Will took a step back and glanced up at Biggs, finding that the normally stoic man had a ghost of a smile on his lips.

"I am warm now, Will," Elizabeth whispered up to him as a warm feeling started in her face and was felt throughout her body. How she wished that Will had kissed her despite the warning, for she had dreamed many a night about his kissing her and more, and this anticipation was driving her to distraction. She regularly dreamed of the man that she loved.

She was not alone in her dreams; the biggest difference was that Will's dreams were far more vivid. He had been innocent until he had visited a courtesan that catered to the very rich while he was on his grand tour. He had only visited her four times, but it was enough to gain an adequate education in the arts of relations between a man and a woman.

"Please accept my deepest apology, Lizzy," Will said, mortified thinking that his almost loss of regulation had upset the woman that he loved.

"You have nothing to apologise for," she returned softly. "I desired the same." Her admission led to her breath feathering in longing.

"You know how I feel about you, do you not, Lizzy?" Will asked as he looked deep into her shining eyes.

"Although we are not allowed to say the words yet, I believe that we are in complete accord on this subject," Elizabeth replied as she held his gaze.

Neither spoke for some minutes, just basking in the comfort of their knowledge until they were reminded of the cold as the wind whipped up and over the crest of Oakham Mount, causing Elizabeth's tresses to be pulled out from under the collar of her coat. "May I escort you back to Longbourn?" Will asked, to which Elizabeth nodded her agreement.

At the base of the hill, with Aggie bounding ahead of them, the couple walked back to Longbourn, trailed by Biggs and Johns, the latter leading Zeus. Words were not required for the looks they gave one another spoke volumes.

~~~~~~~/~~~~~~~

A few days before the Twelfth Night Ball, Will requested the supper and final sets from Elizabeth, which she granted without delay. The only thing that she could repine was that he was only allowed to request two dances.

Much time had been spent on the last-minute details of her coming out ball, which was fast approaching. Elizabeth's mother and Mother Bennet had at last reviewed every detail and finally pronounced the ball planned to their satisfaction.

On the first day of January 1799, Will had the supreme pleasure of consigning the calendar for 1798 to the fire in his chambers. With the first of January already crossed out, there was not much more than a fortnight before he would be dancing with Elizabeth at her ball. His wait was practically over.

He had berated himself for forgetting himself that morning on Oakham Mount even though Elizabeth had acquitted him of any fault in the matter. If Biggs had not cleared his throat, he knew that he would have kissed her, and then the question was, once he did, would he have been able to stop at one? There was no question of him going too far before they were married, as he knew they would be one day. He had discussed his almost kiss with his mother and asked if he needed to tell Andrew.

His mother had opined that as nothing actually happened, he should leave well enough alone. If he had kissed her, then, of course, he would have to tell his cousin. She told him flagellating himself for an action not taken would do nothing, as she was sure he would remember that moment even though there was no understanding between them and would not allow himself to be tempted to give in to his base urges with Elizabeth again.

The day before the Twelfth Night Ball, Elizabeth and Will sat in Longbourn's library reading quietly. Mrs. Annesley was sitting across from them, concentrating on her knitting. "Lizzy," Will called her name softly to gain her attention. "I cannot wait for the time to pass before I am allowed to declare myself for you."

He said as he leaned in toward her to make sure that her companion could not hear his words.

"I too wish it will pass swiftly, Will," Elizabeth responded shyly. "Talking about which, had Andrew given you his choice for when I am allowed to receive any declaration?"

"Yes, he had. He wants you to have the season. He will allow declarations to be made one week before we leave London to avoid the oppressive summer heat," he informed her. "Before your season starts, I also want to own up to there being a time when I was jealous of the attention that Wes was paying you. As much as I would have hated it if he were the one you found your happiness with, I would have withdrawn from the field. Your happiness is the most important thing to me, Lizzy."

"Wes returned to the attention of a family friend once he saw that I did not reciprocate any tender regard, and I believe it was because he noticed that my eyes always sought you out whenever we were in the same room. And," she added, "I did notice the looks that you gave Wes when he paid me attention." She stifled a giggle with her hand as she remembered some of those very deep scowls from that time.

"It pleases me that I was able to provide you such entertainment," he quipped. "I could not help but stare at you, Lizzy. I hope that you know that you are the handsomest lady of my acquaintance, inside and out."

"You are the most handsome man that I know, Will; also one of the best men that I know," Elizabeth blushed as she made the admission. "Do you know that at first, I thought you were looking at me with disapproval or to find fault before I understood the truth?"

"My mother warned me that my intense looks might have been interpreted thusly. It is good that we understand one another now. Misunderstandings and baseless assumptions could have led to superfluous heartache for both of us."

"There is much I would like to say and ask, but I am afraid that we have already come very close to the line Andrew drew between us. Soon Will, soon we will be free to tell one another what is in our hearts," Elizabeth promised softly.

Although the words had not been said or the declarations made, both felt the love that radiated from the other. There were no remaining doubts about if they would be together for the rest of their lives—it was just a question of when. At least Will would have the pleasure of the two dances at the upcoming ball.

~~~~~~~~/~~~~~~~~

Kitty Bennet had pouted when she was informed that she would not be allowed to attend the Twelfth Night Ball. At thirteen, she felt very grown-up, but her mother sat her down and explained that she would not be allowed to attend balls and dances in Meryton until she was sixteen and that it would be a further two years before she would be out in London society.

After her mother's patient explanation, Kitty's attitude had changed for the better, and she had both Mariah Lucas and Cara Long with her for company as they too were not allowed to attend the ball. The three would help look after the family's younger children while James, Tom, Alex, and John Lucas would overnight at Lucas Lodge. At least they had the children, and they had a rousing game of hide and seek planned for them, which they had all loved to play with Jane. Now that Jane was gone, it was time to turn the tide and for them to follow her example so that the same memories they cherished would be passed forward.

As William Bennet readied himself for the ball, he could not believe how fortune had shone on him earlier that day. Had it only been a few short hours ago when the trajectory of his life had shifted on its axis?

William had been invited to meet with Uncle George in his and his Aunt Anne's sitting room. "Please sit," Uncle George indicated an armchair.

"How may I be of assistance, Uncle George?" William asked as he took his seat.

"You graduate from the School of Divinity at Cambridge in April, do you not William?" George Darcy had asked, and William allowed that it was so. "I have spoken to your father, who informed me how

proud he is of your achievements during your studies and that you have been at or near the top of your class consistently. When do you plan to take orders? I know some wait after they complete their studies as they take a grand tour."

"It is my intention to take orders immediately after graduation. Father offered me a grand tour, but I decided that I would like to start doing God's work as soon as I am able." He offered his decision, which he felt was right for him.

"That is what I thought your answer would be. I know that you have spoken to Mr. Pierce about a curacy under him here. Have you made a commitment to him yet?" Mr. Darcy asked easily.

"We have spoken about it, but an offer was not made nor accepted. To what do these questions tend, Uncle George?" William asked, curious about the line of questioning which he could not determine a point to.

"The current rector, Mr. Ignatius Perkins, has notified me that after almost forty years of holding the three livings in my gift, Pemberley, Lambton, and Kympton, that he desires to retire by the end of this year. If you are interested, I would like to offer you a curacy to learn under Mr. Perkins so that you will be able to take over the three livings when he retires." George was amused at how round William's eyes had grown during his explanation and could not quite bite back his smile.

"It is definitely something that I would be interested in, Uncle George, but I do not want to usurp one who had been promised the position. Will told me that his friend Patrick Elliot is a curate at the Lambton church and is in line to receive the livings." William schooled himself to hide the disappointment of not being able to accept.

"I would never make the offer if that were still the fact, regardless of how much I like and respect you. Mr. Elliot was the second son of a baronet from Shropshire. Just this week, I received a note from him that he need to resign his curacy with immediate effect. His brother was killed in a riding accident, so he is required to return to his family's estate as he is now his father's heir. He had already departed by the time the express reached me. I asked if you had an agreement with Mr. Pierce, as if you had, I would not have made you the offer.

"That you would have been willing to step away from such a lucrative group of livings speaks well of your honesty and honour. Besides, I am sure that my niece will not object to having one of her brothers but ten miles distant from Snowhaven," Uncle George had paused. "You do not have to give me an answer now. Talk to your family, for it could be that you do not want to be so far from the rest of the Bennets; however, I would appreciate your answer as soon as you make a decision."

"It is an easy decision for me, Uncle George. We have discussed the possibility that my profession may lead me some distance from Longbourn, and both Father and Mother have told me that they will support me regardless of where I choose to serve God's children. That is a long-winded way of telling you that I gladly accept your offer. You have my undying gratitude for considering me for the position." The two had stood, and William had shaken Uncle George's hand vigorously before leaving to seek out his parents.

As his valet put the finishing touches to his outfit for the ball, William thought about how, when he had found his parents and told them about the position that he would fill after taking his orders, there had been nothing but unstinting support for his decision and a wide grin as his father made mention of having yet another reason to be close to the Pemberley library, and, of course, his second daughter.

~~~~~~~/~~~~~~~

The new Mr. & Mrs. Bingley had returned from Ramsgate the day before the ball and had not yet had time to visit any of their friends and family not living at Netherfield, so the ball was ideal for them. When they walked in, Mrs. Cheryl Long had to check herself not to squeal like a schoolgirl. Her daughter and son-in-law looked most happy as they crossed the dance floor to greet the Long family.

Both of her parents enfolded her in hugs, and Bingley dutifully kissed his mother-in-law on the cheek and shook Mr. Long's hand. Seeing how happy their daughter looked, neither parents doubted that she had a felicitous marriage so far.

Soon after greeting her parents, Mandy Bingley was surrounded by her friends from the neighbourhood. The circle including Jane Rhys-Davies, Franny Phillips, and Charlotte Pierce. Her husband was greeted boisterously by his friends, not least of all was Richard Fitzwilliam, who made not a few off-colour jokes at his friend's newlywed expense.

Elizabeth opened the ball with Richard while Will did the honours with one of the neighbourhood ladies, Miss Goulding, who beamed at being so singled out. "Itch, when we return to Town two days hence, I would like to talk to you," Elizabeth told her brother as they returned to their positions after circling other dancers.

"You know that I can deny you nothing, Lizzy," Richard gave her a half bow as he executed the flawless steps of the dance. "Am I correct that you have tender feelings for that reprobate of a younger cousin of mine?" He surprised his sister with his question.

"I do not believe that this is the time or place for that question, brother!" Elizabeth evaded, her answer in her expressive eyes as she looked up at him.

"That must mean yes," Richard teased. "He is like a brother to me, but if he ever hurts you…"

"He never would," Elizabeth cut her brother off. "You know him too well to suspect it of him."

"You are my baby sister; I have to check!" Richard said almost petulantly.

"I love you too, Itch," Elizabeth said as her rich laughter rang out. It was a sound that the man who loved her and who dancing just a little further down the same line so treasured the hearing that he lit up when it rang out. If Miss Goulding had any doubts that his affections were engaged, his reaction to his cousin's laugh was enough to convince her that he was being kind toward herself, but no hopes should be placed on him.

For both Elizabeth and Will, it was a most enjoyable ball. As they went through the dance steps for the supper set, their eyes were locked one on the other, but for the moments, they were separated by the dance, and when then they seemed to be look-ing for each other all the time. They did not talk during the dance; neither felt the need as they knew what it was all lead-ing to, and the anticipation was there, but the peace which the knowledge brought was most welcome.

As the last bars of the music played, the dancers all applauded the musicians for their stellar playing thus far. Will led Elizabeth to a table where her four brothers sat with their partners. Once she was comfortably seated, he made plates for the both of them. During the meal, when not eating, the two talked softly to one another.

Andrew watched his cousin was being so solicitous toward his baby sister, realizing as he flitted through the memories of their lives that he always was, had always been there for her, and was always thus.

Marie had only danced the supper set with Andrew as she was feeling fatigued. She saw the scowl on her husband's face and understood that it was not one of disapproval of Will but of knowing that his sister would soon be under the protection of another. She distracted her husband with talk of their impend-ing second child, slyly winking at Lizzy, who hid her laugh be-hind a napkin, and then refocused on her own partner. It seemed there was a whole other side she had her first glimpse of in which the women of their family worked together. How fun this would be, and she needed all the help she could get if she was going to get that first kiss soon!

When the first dance of the final set commenced, both Eliza-beth and Will acknowledged its significance. The next time they danced, Elizabeth would be out in society, and not long after, she would have an official suitor, and luckily, she knew who it would be and that she wanted no others.

As Elaine, Tammy, and Anne Darcy sat watching the final dance, Elaine leaned to her sister-in-law. "I believe that we will enjoy sharing a daughter when your son and my daughter finally get to the point."

"If they had their way, it would be sooner rather than later,"

Tammy opined as she watched Elizabeth and Will elegantly execute the steps of the dance.

"I believe that they are the only two that would suit one another," Anne said, agreeing with them, for her son and Elizabeth were lost in each other's eyes. She wondered if they would even hear the music ending without applause to bring back their focus to their surroundings.

There were few who saw them that night that had any doubt that their futures were tightly intertwined. Neither Will nor Elizabeth, had they known, would have cared who knew, as their hearts were overflowing with love, one for the other.

CHAPTER 6

"I appreciate your coming to see me today, Itch," Elizabeth welcomed her brother into her sitting room. She had asked Mrs. Annesley to give them some time while she talked to her brother, so her companion was knitting in a comfortable armchair in Lady Elizabeth's bedchamber.

"As I told you, Sprite, your wish is my command," he gave her a deep bow with a flourish of his bicorn. He kissed Elizabeth's cheeks then sat next to her on the settee. "What is it that we need to discuss, Lizzy? Do I need to take that scoundrel Will to task for you?" he grinned.

"No, Richard, this has nothing to do with Will." As soon as she used his full name, Richard knew that this was a more serious conversation.

"Go to it, Sprite," he invited, his tension increasing for fear that she worried someone again intended her harm.

"You own Brookfield and have since grandmama bequeathed it to you before I joined the family, do you not?" she asked evenly, resting her hand on his to reassure him danger was not afoot.

"What of it?" he asked suspiciously.

"Let me start out by telling you that no one has asked that I talk to you on this subject. Only Marie knows that I am talking to you, and even she does not know the subject I intend," she assured him.

"I will hear what you have to say, Lizzy. More than that, I cannot promise." He covered her hand with his, now holding it between both of his own.

"My request will not come as a surprise, given my opening question," she took a deep breath. "I am *begging* you to sell your commission, resign from the army, and take up the management of your estate."

"You remember when I explained to Father that I felt a calling, Lizzy, that has not changed," he stated, falling silent when she squeezed his hand with hers.

"I know and respect that, Richard, but I put forth to you sometimes men put down their calling to do their duties to their family. Do you remember what Uncle George and Will told us about Mr. Elliot? He had no less of a calling than you, but when the time came to do his duty to his family, he did it without any hesitation." Elizabeth was grateful she had been able to get even this far into the conversation.

"How am I not doing my duty to the family by remaining in the army?" he asked, not seeing the logic of her request.

"Do you have any idea the concern you will cause in Mama or me if you are ever ordered into battle? How much has she already lost? If heaven forbid, she lost you too; she would not recover, Brother. And then there is also how I would be affected." She admitted quietly.

"You? I do not understand?" He scowled.

"My history is known to you better than almost any, Richard, so how can you ask that? Do you think that Mama would be the only one who would not be able to recover if something happened to you? No, it would be me as well. I have lost enough in this life already, Richard," tears began to stream down her cheeks as she spoke, tearing at his heartstrings. "Do you think that I would be able to recover from your loss, especially knowing that you had a choice? How many who have estates and the funds that you have to your name are in the army?" she asked as she wiped her tears away.

"That is a perspective that I will admit I had not yet considered," Richard replied. "Will you give me some days to think about what you have asked of me? The army is a part of me, but," he raised his hand, seeing that she was about to interject, "as I was saying, *but* you, mother, and the family are much larger parts of who I am. So please, Lizzy, give me a little time; this is a life-changing decision.

Elizabeth understood her brother's quandary, so she promised that she would not ask him again before the family dinner after her curtsy before the Queen, which was more than a sennight hence.

On his way back to the Dragoons' barracks, Richard shook his head to clear it. Elizabeth had always had the ability to bring fresh perspectives into relief and had done so again. His father had not stood in his way when he had announced his intention to join the army all those years ago. He knew that neither of his parents was happy about his decision, but they never made their displeasures known to him, thus allowing him to choose his path without interference.

Elizabeth's words haunted him. Could he put his mother, sister, and the rest of the family through that amount of grief that could be avoided if he chose to, especially if he was sent into battle and the worst should happen? He had an option, one that most who chose the army would have jumped at.

Not only did he own an estate, but the profits had been invested for him since he inherited it—the last few years with Gardiner and Associates. He had over one hundred thousand pounds working for him, so he was no poor second son. In fact, he was better off than many first sons.

By the time that he reached his rooms in the barracks, Lieutenant-Colonel Richard Fitzwilliam knew that there was only one decision that he could make. He took a brisk walk across the courtyard to General Atherton's offices and asked the adjutant if the commander was available, and if not, asked for an appointment to see him. As it happened, the General was able to see him.

Richard saluted smartly and was shown to a seat by the Royal Dragoons' commanding general. "Yes, Colonel," General Atherton drawled.

"I have reached a very painful decision sir, I am going to resign from the army and sell my commission," Richard informed his superior officer.

"Why now Colonel Fitzwilliam?" he was asked. He relayed the conversation that he had with his younger sister and sheepishly informed the shocked man that he was no poor second son but a man of independent means.

"You joined the army while at the same time you owned an estate that cleared more than eight thousand a year?" Richard nodded. "I honour your patriotism, but why? Most of us who choose the army do so because we need to. You did not."

"No sir, I did not, but I felt that it was my calling," Richard explained.

"That is understandable, and you made one fine head of the training grounds, but as much as I hate to lose an officer like yourself, I can see your sister's point of view. Fill out the paperwork, and I will accept your resignation. There will be no shortage of potential purchasers for a lieutenant-colonel's commission." Atherton stood, as did Richard. Richard saluted, and the General returned it.

The adjutant handed Richard the required form, and once his name was affixed to it, the form was placed in front of General Atherton, who signed it. In three days' time, Lieutenant-Colonel Richard Fitzwilliam would no longer be a member of His Majesty's Army. He decided that he would not inform his family until his resignation was final after the General who was chief of personnel signed the form.

He had thought about taking this step several times but had always convinced himself that this was what he really wanted. All it took was fifteen minutes with Elizabeth to make him look at things again and come to a quite different conclusion. He did not know a lot about estate management, but he did know that Andrew, Will, and Uncle George would be beyond excited to teach him, and besides, his steward at Brookfield, Mr. Murray Lefroy, was excellent at what he did and as honest as the day was long.

~~~~~~~/~~~~~~~

As the day of her curtsy approached, Elizabeth could feel her excitement building. She had worked with her mother, Marie, and Mrs. Annesley until she could execute the curtsey and the backing away from the Queen flawlessly. Elizabeth detested the dress with the hoops, train, and layers which she would have to wear for her presentation, which fulfilled the very strict dictates in design from the palace, which had not changed for many decades. She had practiced in her mother's old one and had tripped more than once as she learnt how to walk and back away in the monstrosity.

Besides practicing for her presentation, much time had been spent at Mrs. Chambourg's shop on the gown she would wear for her coming out ball, along with a completely new wardrobe that would be needed for one now in society, after which there had been much shopping for all of the accoutrements that she would require. Unlike most young ladies, shopping was not high on the list of things that Elizabeth preferred to do. It was something that she tolerated but truly did not enjoy.

The ball gown was made of rich burgundy silk with a clear gossamer overlay that had diamond chips sewn into it that would reflect the light as she walked, giving the effect of twinkling stars. The sleeves ended just above her elbow, and the gown flared out from the empire waist and had a lower cut neckline, more daring than anything that Elizabeth had ever owned before. She had ensured that it was not too low cut as some wore, even though she had ample assets to fill the bust line of the gown. When she tried it on for the final fitting, it made her feel like a fairy princess, and there was only one prince that she saw in her mind's eye.

Elizabeth was sponsored by her mother but was also accompanied to St. James Palace by Jane, Marie, and Tammy Bennet. When the Lord Chamberlain announced "Lady Elizabeth Rose Bennet Fitzwilliam," all of the courtiers in the reception chamber quieted. Many had not seen Lady Elizabeth for some years and were struck by the absolute beauty that made her way towards the Queen.

Elizabeth executed a flawless curtsey, then expected the queen to proffer her hand to kiss as was done for the daughter of an earl. Instead, Queen Charlotte beckoned her closer to her throne and kissed Elizbeth on the forehead as she would the daughter of a duke.

"We are most pleased that you are entering society, Lady Elizabeth," the Queen intoned kindly.

"I thank you for your acknowledgement, your royal majesty," Elizabeth returned softly.

"We hope that you will have time to come visit our husband and us at Buckingham House to play and sing for us, Lady Elizabeth; we are related after all," the Queen stated.

"When your majesty desires my presence, it will be my honour." Seeing the little wave of her majesty's hand indicating that she was dismissed, Elizabeth backed away without tripping and re-joined her family in the antechamber. She was hugged by all four of the ladies who had accompanied her to the palace.

"Welcome to society, Lizzy," her mother smiled. Elaine felt ambivalence, she was as proud as any mother could be in her daughter, but at the same time, she knew that this was a further step away from the family she had grown up with while being a step toward her future family. There was no doubt in Elaine's mind that when her daughter married, she would often see her, especially as all signs indicated that she would be moving only ten miles away.

"Thank you, Mama," Elizabeth replied. She too had mixed emotions this day, but hers were predominately happy now that she was out, though she was not overjoyed, as there were still almost five months before Will would be allowed to declare himself. She had a plan. After her eighteenth birthday, a full two months from her coming-out ball, she would ask her brother for the birthday gift that she desired above all others.

"You did so well; what did her majesty say to you, Lizzy?" Tammy asked.

"Thank you, Mother Bennet, especially for all the help and training, so I was prepared. She will be inviting me to come perform for her at Buckingham House soon," Elizabeth reported. To some, a royal summons would be nerve-racking, but to one who had been giving musical performances to the royals for well over ten years, it was almost routine.

"Let us return to Matlock House; the newest member-to-be of the Fitzwilliam family demands that I rest," Marie stated, and with that request, the five ladies departed the palace.

~~~~~~~/~~~~~~~

On walking into the drawing room at Matlock House, Elizabeth saw Richard and was about to jump into his arms as was her wont when she stopped herself in her tracks. "Itch, where is your uniform?" she asked suspiciously, hoping that what she suspected was true.

"Did I not promise you that I would convey my answer to you before your ball, Sprite?" he asked with a broad smile. "I am now the Honourable Mr..." He did not have a chance to finish what he was about to say as his sister launched herself into his arms, hoops and all.

"You are no longer in the army! This is the best gift you have ever bestowed on any of us, Itch!" Elizabeth got out as she hugged her brother tightly.

Elaine stood with tears of joy streaming down her cheek. "You have made your mother very happy, Richard," she informed him as she waited for her daughter to detach herself from her brother so that she could hug her second son. "Your father and I always hoped that you would sell out and take up the life of a gentleman. My Reggie would have been as happy as I am if he were still here to see this day."

"Lizzy gave me a lot to think on, and for once," he teased his sister, "she made sense. "As of this morning, I am a civilian, my resignation is official, and there is a buyer for my commission."

"In that case, we will have to toast Itch at dinner tonight," Elizabeth decided.

"It is your night, Lizzy, not mine," Richard stated.

"As it is my night, my desire is to toast the master of Brookfield, the best of brothers!" Elizabeth gave Richard a look he had seen many times, an arched eyebrow daring him to gainsay her.

"Andrew, you do not look very surprised," Marie pointed out.

"I had to tell someone, and as all of you like surprises so much, we decided to give you one," Richard shared while Andrew had a happy, smug look that told of his success in surprising Elizabeth, who was normally not easy to surprise.

~~~~~~~/~~~~~~~

Bennet House was awash with the light of what seemed to be a thousand candles as the guests for the celebratory dinner arrived. The Phillipses and Gardiners arrived together earlier than the rest of the guests, as planned so that the family could toast the newest member of society. Ian and Anne Ashby had already arrived in support of their sister as they were staying at the newly named Ashby House on Berkley Square.

Georgiana, at almost fifteen, was most happy that she could attend the formal dinner. As it was only family and close friends, her not being out had been overlooked by her mother, especially as Elizabeth had requested her friend be allowed to attend.

"Was it as scary as they say it is, Lizzy?" Georgiana asked her cousin.

"If one practices well beforehand, then, in my opinion, the presentation is not something to fear, Gigi," Elizabeth informed the younger girl. "My only worry was the backing out. Even though I had practiced many times, I imagined myself falling on my derriere and making a spectacle, but that did not happen." The vision that her cousin described caused a giggle from Georgiana, who covered her mouth in an attempt to hide her reaction, but her eyes gave it away.

Elizabeth had not seen Will yet, but without turning, she knew he was behind her. She could detect his cologne of sandalwood and spices that she liked so much. She was in much anticipation for her ball when she would dance with him for the first time as a full member of society.

For his part, Will was taking in Elizabeth's lavender scent. Only two more days to cross off, and then he would dance with her at her ball. They had danced before, as recently as the Twelfth Night Ball, but none had the significance of the dances that he would have at the coming out, and never had they danced with the full glare of the Ton's attention on them. There would be no doubt as to his preference afterward.

Andrew and Bennet offered toasts to honour Elizabeth. In Andrew's toast, among other things, he talked about how he could not believe that the little whirlwind that had blown through their houses for so many years was the poised and elegant young lady standing before him as he welcomed his sister as a full member of society.

Bennet's highlighted his and the rest of the Bennet's joy at being part of Elizabeth's life and how much joy reuniting with her had brought all of them. He was sure, he said, that whoever was lucky enough to one day win her heart would have to be a very worthy man. During that part of the toast, he had looked at Will.

Not long after, the De Melville's and Ian's parents and sister Amy arrived. Richard had never paid attention to Lady Loretta de Melville before, thanks to the limited time that he was able to spend with the family during his army service, so he had missed most of her visits. The lady had come out the previous season, and, as far as he knew, she had no suitor.

She had grown into a very pretty and poised young lady who, from the snippets of conversation that Richard could hear, was intelligent and witty, not another vapid debutant with air between her ears. He made the decision to try to get to know her, to see if she would pique his interest and if he would rouse hers.

Luckily for Richard, he was placed opposite the lady at dinner and had the pleasure of escorting her to the table, while his cousin Will had the pleasure of escorting Elizabeth in, although he was disappointed that he was not sitting next to her. As the guest of honour, she was seated to her birth father's right with Marie next to her. Even not being directly opposite his love, he did have a good view of her from where he sat next to Jane and Perry. It was hard to miss the furtive looks that passed between the two during the meal; those caught in the middle were more amused than annoyed as they occasionally intentionally got in the way to engage one or the other in a conversation neither wanted to have.

As they had before their friends arrived, both Andrew and

Bennet toasted Elizabeth's entrance into society, and after the clinking and 'hear hears' subsided, Andrew made an announcement: "It gives me great pleasure to inform all here that, as of today, Lizzy's brother Richard Fitzwilliam is no longer in the army. Please join me in toasting the Honourable Mr. Richard Fitzwilliam and wishing him well in his endeavours managing his estate." Richard accepted the well wishes of the assembled company gratefully.

During the separation of the sexes, Jane asked her younger sister to join her in a corner where they were not close to any of the other ladies. With Georgiana's playing the pianoforte, they were assured that others would not hear them.

"Lizzy, do you and Will have an understanding?" Jane asked directly.

"Not officially," Elizabeth replied coyly.

"Did he ask for your hand before you were out?" Jane probed.

"No, Jane, he has not. There is no secret courtship or betrothal —yet. If he had asked, I would have accepted him regardless of what everyone else wishes, but Andrew was clear with the timing of any declarations, and Will has not contravened Andrew's dictates," Elizabeth replied. "It is the end of the season that has been set as the time the restrictions will be lifted, although I plan to ask Andrew for a very special birthday gift."

"If he has not declared himself, what do you mean by 'not officially'?"

"We have discussed issues in generalities, so the understanding that we have is that we both desire the time we can say the words we very much want to say. I love him, Jane. I love him more than I knew it was possible to love another." Elizabeth met her sister's assessment without hesitation and nodded when Jane nodded slowly that she knew and saw the truth.

"He will make you a good husband, Lizzy. I look forward to being able to call him brother." Jane hugged her sister.

"How are you feeling with your state, Jane?" Elizabeth changed the subject.

"Much better than I expected. I know that many feel sick in

the mornings by the third month, but I have been well so far. There are some smells that I can no longer tolerate, but luckily I have experienced no aversion to any foods yet," Jane informed her sister.

"Do your mother or mother-in-law suspect that you are with child?" Elizabeth smiled as she believed they probably did if how quickly Marie's state was suspected was any indication.

"Possibly, but neither has asked me anything directly regarding pregnancy yet. I believe they are waiting for me to talk to them. According to the accoucheur, I saw who confirmed my state, I should feel the quickening in the next month or so, then Perry and I will make the announcement." Jane nodded, loving anew that she was talking about her child with her sister Lizzy.

Not long after, the men joined the women, and the party was treated to exhibitions of musical talent by the ladies. Lady Anne, who rarely played in public anymore, displayed her prodigious talent. Richard was impressed by the proficiency Lady Loretta displayed, and, as was usual, Elizabeth closed the evening with her magnificent playing accompanied with a song that closed the evening on the perfect note of pleasure.

CHAPTER 7

Fitzwilliam Darcy crossed out the date circled with three red circles on his calendar. He was tempted to circle the date in June that would allow him to declare himself, but he decided against it. Now that Elizabeth was out, he could behave in ways that would not have been acceptable before she had done so without crossing the line that Andrew had set.

He had no idea what her gown would look like, but Will was sure that she would look gorgeous in it regardless of the style of dress. There would be a family reception with the two royals, then the receiving line, and then the ball would commence. He was alive with anticipation of the pleasure of his three dances with her as it was the start of his quest in earnest.

When the Darcys crossed the square to Matlock's house, they met the Bennets, Gardiners, and Phillipses walking toward the same house. Georgiana, Kitty, and Lilly Gardiner were accompanying their parents. They would be allowed to see Elizabeth in her dress, and they would then be escorted to Bennet House, where all the younger children of the family would spend the night.

Thénardier was just putting the finishing touches on her mistress's coiffure when Andrew knocked on the door and entered holding a velvet-covered box in his hands. "What is that Andrew?" Elizabeth was very curious as she had not expected more on top of all else that had been purchased.

"Part of the Matlock jewels, Sprite. I am not sure if I may still call you that now that you are out, Lizzy," Andrew said, as he beheld the girl that was now a woman before him.

He opened the box, and Elizabeth saw the most magnificent necklace of alternating diamonds and rubies, which got larger until they reached a huge ruby in the centre. There was a tiara in the same stones and diamond and ruby earbobs. Elizabeth watched in fascination as her maid placed the jewels on her person. When her lady's maid had finished the task, she could not believe that the lady in the mirror was herself. Andrew extended his arm, and she placed her gloved hand delicately on his forearm, then they walked toward the grand staircase.

"*C'est très bien,*" Thénardier said quietly as she watched her mistress descend the stairs.

The Darcy and Bennet parties were just divesting themselves of their outerwear when Elizabeth descended the stairs on her brother's arm. Will's mouth hung open as the vision descended the stairs, and he tracked her every movement. It was only when he felt Georgiana's elbow connect with his ribs gently and heard her soft giggle that he closed his gaping mouth as his sister's action pulled him out of his trance.

He had always known that Elizabeth was beautiful, but this was beyond anything that he had envisioned. She was stunning. He was happy she would be dancing with so many men from the family as it ensured she would not have many dances open for potential rivals. It was then that he reminded himself that she was not fickle and that even dancing with every eligible bachelor in London would not change her feelings for him.

As Elizabeth and Andrew reached the bottom step, Jane, Perry, and Aunt Rose entered the foyer. "We have all seen Lizzy before; should we not adjourn to the drawing room?" Richard smirked. He would have to use all his military training backing up the men in the family to make sure that no one stepped out of line with his baby sister that night.

As Andrew watched the look on Will's face as he escorted his sister down the stairs, he smiled, knowing that her heart very much belonged to Will. His late father had always spoken about the age of eighteen, and in a way, Andrew's stipulation to wait until June was a nod to the late earl; however, as all present now knew, Lizzy would be eighteen in March. He had fought against acceptance of the fact his little sister, the one he called Sprite, was no longer a little girl. She was, in fact, a young woman in love. Letting go of the privilege of her day-to-day protection would not be easy, but he would do it. After all, he wanted his sister to be happy, and she had clearly decided that Will made her happy.

Anne and Ian, accompanied by the Earl and Countess of Ashbury, arrived just before the toasts. After the toasts, Anne cornered her brother Richard and asked him why he had decided to resign from the Army at this time; he told her about his conversation with Lizzy. Anne felt a great debt of gratitude to her sister, as she understood her younger sister was one of the only people who could reach Richard and cause him to consider the path he had taken.

Lady Elaine announced that it was time to form the receiving line as the first guests would be arriving soon. The line would consist of Andrew, Marie, Elaine, Elizabeth, Bennet, and finally, Tammy. Richard did not repine the fact that he was not part of the receiving line, for then he was on hand to greet the De Melville's right after they cleared the line of arriving guests.

"Good evening, Lady Loretta," he bowed over the lady's hand after he had greeted her family.

"Mr. Fitzwilliam," she returned, amused at his pointed address.

"If you have a set open for an ex-soldier, I would like to write my name down, should you grant me that honour," he requested gallantly. The more he talked to her, the more he liked Loretta De Melville, for her hint of amusement proved she saw through him and his hope to claim her hand.

"As you can see, I am dancing the first with my brother and the one before the supper set with my father, but the rest are open," she informed him boldly.

Richard wrote his name into the space opposite the supper set, then held the pencil above the final set and looked at the lady questioningly. She gave him an almost imperceptible nod, and he smiled privately at her in appreciation as he claimed the final set. He was sure that she would have granted him a third set, but not having cleared such a request with her father before the ball, he decided not to ask.

Once all the guests were present, Prince Edward and Princess Elizabeth entered to bows and curtsies from all. At a nod from the Earl of Matlock, the musicians played a few bars of music to signal the commencement of the dancing and the first set. As had been planned, the Prince led Lady Elizabeth to the head of the line. With another signal from Lord Matlock, the music started. The Prince danced a few bars with his partner, and then Andrew replaced him.

"You have grown into a wonderful young lady, Lizzy," Andrew told her as the steps of the dance brought them together.

"Thank you, Andrew; you are one of the best brothers that a girl could ask for. I am just sorry that Papa is not here dancing with me tonight," she replied wistfully.

"You and me both, Lizzy, you and me both." At the end of the first dance of the set, Bennet took over the duties from Andrew.

"This is still like a dream for me, Lizzy," Bennet said.

"How so, Father Bennet?" she asked.

"It is so much more than I ever dared to hope. All I prayed for was that you were well cared for and loved. Not only was that true, beyond anything I prayed for, but I, we the Bennets, are a part of your life. Look how much family we have gained." The dance parted them as they went down the line.

"As hard as it must have been for you when I was stolen, I would not trade the life I have had so far for anything as I have been loved and cared for by parents and a family who always protected me. If I had never been taken and discarded, I would have been happy to grow up with my birth family, but it seems that God had other plans for us all. Most people dream of one loving family; I have many." The line separated them one more time, and when they were back together, Elizabeth completed her thought. "Now I am embarking on a new part of my life, and, when my wish is granted, I will become a part of a family who I already love, but I will always have all of my family with me in my heart even when I do not see you." When the dance was over,

Bennet was too choked up with emotion to talk, so her kissed his second daughter on the forehead and led her to her next partner, who was eagerly awaiting her.

As Will led Elizabeth to the head of the line for the second set, they were lost in each other's eyes and had no idea who lined up next to them. It was Andrew and Marie who were amused at the two of them being so transfixed on one another, as no one present could miss the loving looks passing between the two. When the music commenced, there was companionable silence between the two at the head of the line for the first ten minutes.

"Come now, Lady Elizabeth," Will teased the lady he loved, "we must have some conversation; think of the gossip it will excite if we are silent the whole half hour."

"Do you normally talk when you dance?" she challenged, her playful smile making him grin.

"I could comment on the number of people present, and you could mention how well the ballroom is decorated," he re-joined, his dimples in evidence.

"We can discuss anything that your heart desires, Mr. Darcy. Would you like to discuss a book, perchance?" She volleyed, anxiously awaiting his reply.

"No, my Lady, discussing books while dancing is not the done thing," he scoffed, his eyes lighting up at the wordplay she so naturally fell into with him.

Were they cognisant of others in the room, they would have seen the astonishment of the Ton as they watched two for whom the rest of the world seemed not to exist. It was whispered in more than one corner that they had never known the Darcy heir had dimples, or even that he could smile beyond a perfunctory thin allowance for appearance's sake, all and sundry now seeing what none outside of the family had ever seen from the normally stoic, sometimes dour man. When whatever they were discussing caused a tinkling laugh from the lady, the gentleman's face was said to brighten, and he would smile anew.

Several members of the Ton watching them understood two things—neither Lady Elizabeth nor Mr. Fitzwilliam Darcy would ever become part of their family, and the mask that the latter had previously displayed in public was just that, a mask to keep unwanted attention at bay.

It was no surprise for the family members of the two that they had known for many years that the two were formed for one another. Lady Elaine, Lady Rose, and Lady Anne were sitting together watching not only Lizzy and Will, but their Richard, who was longingly watching Lady Loretta as she danced.

"I have a feeling that it will not be too much longer before I have no unmarried children left," Elaine opined. Her sister Anne commiserated with her.

"Since when has Richard been interested in Loretta?" Lady Rose asked as she watched him watch her.

"That is news to me. I was unaware that he was captivated by any lady," Elaine admitted. "If it comes to pass, they will do well together. She is vivacious and intelligent and will always keep him on his toes."

"Have you noted that my daughter-in-law has been resting a lot lately? She and Perry are sitting after dancing the first; do you think that mayhap she is with child?" Lady Rose asked as she looked at Jane and Perry.

"You see them more than we do," Anne replied, "I am sure if she is, we will all be informed when they feel it is the time to do so."

"Speaking about being with child, Marie shared with us that she felt the quickening of our second grandchild a few days ago," Lady Rose offered this next happy topic with a smile, and her friends confirmed they had been privy to the news as well, as the men of their family were ever so fond of sending an express.

When the dance ended, Will reluctantly led Elizabeth back to her brothers. At least the next dance was with Richard rather than someone unknown. Will checked his jealousy as he reminded himself that he had naught to worry about, turning to search for Lady Loretta, with who he would partner for the third set.

When they danced the supper set, neither Elizabeth nor Will

felt the need for conversation. All that needed to be shared was said with but a shared glance or prolonged look, for there were times when words did not adequately express what needed to be said. At last, they could share it, one to the other.

Further down the line, Richard was enjoying his first dance with Lady Loretta. She moved very gracefully, and he acknowledged to himself for the first time that he had started to develop tender feelings for the lady. He did not know how she felt, but he strongly believed that fortune favours the brave and that he would soon request an audience with her to request a courtship. He had no doubt that with her forthright nature that should she not believe their future happiness included the two of them, then she would not accept a courtship as they would be seated together for the meal when he intended to request her permission to call on her on the morrow.

Before the revellers made their way to the bountiful supper that was ready for them, the Prince and Princess departed to the expected courtesies from the crowd. Will led Elizabeth to a table where they were joined by Jane and Perry, Andrew and Marie, Richard and Loretta, and Wes and his partner. After verifying their ladies' preferences, the men went to make plates.

After his supper partner had put her knife and fork down, thereby indicating that she was sated, Richard leaned close to Loretta so only she would hear him. "May I call on you tomorrow, or would you prefer to recover from the ball and have me call the following day?" he asked with bated breath.

"Tomorrow at eleven would suit very well, Mr. Fitzwilliam, and I will receive your call with pleasure," she stated with a light blush as she demonstrated her joy at his request. Richard grinned as he settled into relief, her response exactly what he had hoped for. He was sure that she was not indifferent to him, and he was now looking forward to the final set with much anticipation.

Will also was very much looking forward to the final set. After he had led Elizabeth to the floor for the supper set, any who tried to tell themselves that they had misread the signs they had seen during the first time the two danced had to admit that they were fooling themselves. None had *ever* seen the Darcy heir dance more than one set at a London event prior to this night.

Elizabeth danced with some men, not of her family, between the sets that she relished with Will. No matter what any of the men, some of them dandies, tried to say to impress her about their wealth or connections, she forced herself to keep a neutral look on her visage despite the inherent distastefulness. In each case, she could not wait for the set to end so she could escape the man with alacrity.

When the final set was called, Will led Elizabeth out, and Richard followed with Loretta. The tongues that had been wagging before now reached a fever pitch, but it was the Countess of Jersey who had the most surprised smile. Her daughter had informed her that she had tender feelings for Richard Fitzwilliam; she had held him in high esteem for some years and was happy he seemed to be paying attention to her as a lady and not just one of his sister's friends. It seemed he had finally opened his eyes and was about to make her daughter the happiest of young ladies in the room, perhaps even more so than Elizabeth, as they had all known that outcome for years.

"You know you will not be able to make them wait until June before they reach an understanding, do you not, my love?" Marie consoled her husband as he watched his younger cousin guide his sister down the line.

"I am aware of that, Marie. I will say nothing until one of them brings it up, but if I were to wager, it would be our sister who raises the issue," Andrew opined prophetically.

As Will led Elizabeth back to where her brothers and mother waited for her, he squeezed her hand. "I had the best time tonight, Will," Elizabeth stated, "especially my three sets with you."

"They were the highlights of the evening for me as well, Lizzy," Will promised. "Unless you found one of the dandies that squired you for a dance to be your preference," he grinned.

"Well, there was Lord so-and-so that kept on about the size of his assets. He was most—gauche, so impressive that I choose not to recall his name. Alas, no, you are safe, Will. There is only one who holds my interest," she declared while holding his eyes. The two were so lost in each other they did not notice that they were standing on the dance floor alone.

"Ahem," Andrew cleared his throat as the family looked on in amusement. "I believe it is time for you to return home, Will, and I do not want to see you here before midday later today!" Andrew ribbed his cousin.

The spell was broken as the two realised that they were not alone, both embarrassed as they looked at their amused joint families. After some farewells, the Fitzwilliams finally retired with Elizabeth's head full of the man who she loved. In her wildest dreams, she could not have imagined a more enjoyable coming out ball. She felt lassitude after dancing every set, but it was the best kind of weariness she had ever experienced.

In his chambers, Richard could scarcely sleep at all, occasionally pacing the length of his chambers to relieve his need for action. In a matter of hours, he would know if he would be accepted or rejected; and while he had a feeling that it was the former, he would not make assumptions. He finally fell asleep with thoughts of Lady Loretta De Melville's soft smile in response to his request to call, clinging to its promise.

CHAPTER 8

Richard presented his card to the butler at Jersey House precisely five minutes before the appointed hour and was shown into the Earl of Jersey's study. Lord Cyril De Melville welcomed Richard and indicated that he should sit.

"What are your intentions towards my daughter, Mr. Fitzwilliam?" the Earl asked without preamble.

"Entirely honourable, my Lord. With your leave, it is my intention to request a courtship when I meet with Lady Loretta," Richard responded evenly.

"I am aware that you have a healthy income both from your estate and the years of profits that were invested while you served King and Country. Hence, I am confident that your interest in my daughter is not mercenary. Are you aware of the size of her dowry?" the Earl tested.

"I am not, my Lord, but whatever it is, it will be the least attractive trait that I admire in your daughter. As you rightly pointed out, between my estate and investments, I have more than enough income to keep your daughter in the style to which she is accustomed to. My combined income is more than fifteen thousand clear per annum," Richard stated plainly.

The Earl was impressed; his income was significantly higher than rumoured. "Loretta has five and thirty thousand as her dowry."

"If our courtship progresses to the conclusion that I hope that it will, and your daughter accepts me, the settlement will leave control of her dowry to her, besides my being able to settle a similar amount on her," Richard informed the Earl.

The truth was, although determined to put the second Fitzwilliam through an inquisition, the Earl knew that there was no one better suited to his daughter. But in addition to his own belief, he and his wife had discussed how his late friend Reggie would have been so happy at a familial connection between the families. He was aware that Wes had been enamoured of Lady Elizabeth, but he had backed away when he had noticed the said lady had a clear preference elsewhere.

"If you wait here, Richard, I will summon Loretta. The door will, of course, remain half-open." With that, Lord Jersey stood and shook his daughter's suitor's hand.

Richard relaxed. He knew when the Earl had reverted to his informal name that he had won his approval to court and marry his beloved daughter. It was but a minute or two before Lady Loretta entered; the door was left half-open as her father indicated. They were limited to five minutes to speak privately.

"You came, Mr. Fitzwilliam," she said as she sat opposite him, and when she was settled, Richard sat so they could easily converse.

"Nothing would have kept me away, Lady Loretta. I have a question to ask you, an important one, by your leave." He held his breath as he searched her eyes to ensure she was being as open with him as he was with her.

"I am here to listen to you. But can we revert to our informal names? We have known one another for many years." Loretta smiled, allowing him to look as deep as he dared. One day, hopefully soon, he would realize how long it had taken him to come to the point, but she would let him make it up to her for the rest of their lives.

"In that case, Loretta, I have to tell you that I have developed tender feelings for you. I no longer see you as just a friend of Lizzy's, but as someone who I believe will one day be the ideal helpmate for me. I have been many years in the army and little in society, so I request the honour of a formal courtship," Richard asked with feeling.

"It would be my absolute pleasure to grant you a courtship, Richard. Just like you have for me, I have developed tender feelings for you; for me, it has been of some duration. It may not be love yet, but I believe the courtship will assist us in clarifying those feelings," she responded with pleasure.

"I thank you for accepting my courtship, Loretta; you have made me a happy man today. If and or when the courtship progresses so the next question can be asked, I will be the happiest of men. I need to speak with your father." Richard lifted each of her hands, turned them over, and bestowed a kiss on each wrist.

"Let me request his presence," Loretta stood with an enhanced glow of happiness about her. Her father walked in almost as soon as she exited, letting Richard know his decision only to kiss her hands had been the prudent one, as the Earl had obviously been close by.

"Loretta, Lady Loretta, has done me the great honour of accepting my offer for a courtship, my Lord. I now request your consent, and hopefully your blessing," Richard stood up tall, his happiness too complete to fully hide his smile, even out of respect for her father.

"'Loretta' is fine, Richard; it has been many years since there has been any formality between our families. You have my consent and unequivocal blessing. I am only sorry that my friend Reggie is not with us to see this day," Lord Cyril stood and shook Richard's hand again as his voice strained with emotion.

"Thank you, my Lord. I will always treat your daughter as she deserves to be treated; her happiness will always be my most important duty," Richard replied emphatically.

Lord Jersey led Richard into the drawing room, where he and Loretta received the best wishes from her mother and brother.

~~~~~~~/~~~~~~~

As they all suspected, the gossip rags that morning were full of information from, as they termed it, 'the ball of the season.' Besides the debutante's gown and jewels, the main topic of discussion was that not only did FD of P from Derbyshire smile in public, but he danced three times with the gorgeous Lady EF.

The writer of the on-dit opined that there should be no doubts, after seeing the mooncalf looks that each gave the other, that both were firmly off the marriage mart.

When the Earl of Granville read the piece, he was most displeased. He needed one with a dowry of the size that lady Elizabeth's was reputed to have to save the ancestral home that he had all but lost at the tables. An infusion of cash was necessary to keep the debt collectors away.

Lord Harry Smythe was desperate, and men in his position very seldom thought clearly.

~~~~~~~/~~~~~~~

Matlock House had been inundated with gentlemen callers the morning after the ball, with some who obviously were wilfully blind, ignoring the fact that the lady had demonstrated a noticeably clear preference for but one man at her ball. The callers included the dandy that Elizabeth had aptly dubbed Lord so-and-so. He and all the others were given a clear and coherent message that even the most obtuse among them could grasp when they were informed that the lady was not at home to callers.

As the last two departed, they did not miss Fitzwilliam Darcy being welcomed warmly into the house. The word was soon disseminated that one would be wasting his time if he called at Matlock House with the intent to call on Lady Elizabeth. Thankfully for the said lady, the message was understood by most of the dandies and fortune hunters alike. Of those who had thoughts of trying to compromise the lady, they were quickly abandoned as they knew that if they even attempted such an ill-advised action, they would have to deal with Richard Fitzwilliam. Even the bravest among them was not willing to take *that* chance. There were; however, a few determined fortune hunters among the Ton who would chance anything to get their hands on her rumoured to be large dowry.

Andrew, who had come to a decision since his head hit his pillow a few hours earlier, asked for his cousin to be shown into his study. After Will sat, Andrew took a breath and then spoke. "I know that I had previously said that you would not be allowed to declare yourself until June, but the feeding frenzy this morning has made me reconsider my position." Seeing his cousin's visage light up, he held up his hand. "I am well aware that neither of you needs a courtship to decide if you are meant for one another, but that is all I will allow for now. It will be a clear message to the fortune hunters that they would be wasting their time and trying to compromise her will gain them nothing."

"When will I be allowed to propose to Lizzy?" Will asked.

"Once she turns eighteen, you may propose. Before you ask, I require a minimum of a three-month betrothal. I will not countenance any talk of a rushed wedding," Andrew stated firmly. Will knew the conditions were not open to negotiation, so he accepted them without argument; for now, he could claim his Lizzy, would be able to hold her hand in public, would be able to dance thrice with her at any ball, would be able to keep her close enough to touch, even if propriety dictated that he could not actually do so.

"I will ask Lizzy to join you, Will," Andrew stated as he stood. "Just remember to always make her happy," her brother warned as he went to seek out his sister.

"Will? Why did Andrew allow us to have a private interview with the study door partially closed?" Elizabeth walked toward the settee, an arched brow the only indication that she was not confused. She had overdone her irritation at the callers intentionally, and her mother had had a hard time keeping a straight face through some of it; Marie did not even try the poor souls.

"It is because I am allowed to ask you a question." Will saw Elizabeth's face light up just as his had when Andrew had given permission. "Not *that* question," Will explained what he had been told and the time restrictions. "Lady Elizabeth Rose Bennet Fitzwilliam, will you make me the happiest of men and enter a formal courtship with me until the fifth day of March this year?"

"Yes, oh yes, I will absolutely grant you a formal courtship," Elizabeth replied breathlessly, feeling as if she could float on the wings of happiness. She stood, in need of some action, and despite wanting to fling herself into his arms, did not, but just barely was able to hold herself in check. Darcy chuckled as he stood with her, unwilling to allow so much space between then when he no longer was required to.

"You must allow me to tell you how ardently I love you, Lizzy, and I cannot wait until you become my wife and we are never parted again," Darcy murmured as he looked down into her eyes, his hand holding hers as tightly as she held his.

"I love you too, Will, more than I ever imagined it was possible to love the man that I want to marry." She promised softly.

Darcy was transfixed by her, unconsciously leaning down toward her until she licked her lips in invitation. He glanced up into her eyes to verify she knew his intention and would grant him this gift. Unlike the time on Oakham Mount where they stopped themselves, his lips brushed against hers. It was a chaste kiss, but her feathered exhale was the promise of so much more. Will ached to kiss her again, but he did not want to give Andrew cause to repine his decision.

Just as they stepped away from one another, there was a knock on the door, and Andrew entered before he received an answer. "Is there something you need to ask me, Will?" he asked, knowing full well that his sister accepted the courtship.

"Lizzy has done me the honour of accepting a courtship. We request…" Andrew cut him off before he completed his request.

"Considering that I was the one that gave permission for you to ask, you know you both have my consent, but I want you to know you have my blessing. For some reason, your family arrived while you were talking to this Sprite," Andrew shared. "A little bird must have told them that there would be news to share, but before we go talk to them, there is one more from whom you must get consent, Will." Bennet stepped into the study.

It was a short interview for Bennet had long known the outcome of their story as assuredly as he had for any book he had read, and Elizabeth's birth father added his consent and blessing. He and Andrew revealed that they had spoken an hour earlier when Andrew called on Bennet House and shared his thoughts with Bennet and Tammy. They had agreed that the plan was an excellent way to protect Elizabeth from unwanted attention.

As the four entered the drawing room where the three families waited, Richard and the De Melvilles were announced. Elizabeth did not miss the look of happiness on her brother's face. "Itch? Is there something that you need to tell us?" she asked suspiciously.

"Yes," responded Richard in confusion. He did not miss the trays with champagne flutes ready on the sideboard, nor the expectant looks on everyone's faces. "Wait, how did you know I would have news like this?"

"This was not for your news," Andrew said as he looked pointedly at his sister and Will, who were standing next to one another with bemused expressions.

"Lizzy and Will? I thought not before June?" Richard frowned.

"I will explain after we toast them, and it seems you as well," Andrew stated. "I was about to announce that Lizzy and Will have entered into a formal courtship. What is your news, brother?"

"That was to be my and Lord Jersey's announcement as well," Richard informed the gathering, although no one doubted that was the case as he had unconsciously reached out and twined his hands with Loretta, who beamed as she looked up at him. His clear preference and hope for closeness were a tell no one could fake; she had often seen her father reach for her mother thusly.

"In that case, we have a double celebration." Andrew proposed a toast to Lizzy and Will, which Lord Cyril followed with one for Loretta and Richard. For those not privy to his reasoning, Andrew explained why he had changed his mind on the timing. He revealed that he would have granted a request to shorten his deadline to his sister's birthday if he had been asked, which caused Elizabeth to give Will a smug 'I told you so' look.

Given the logic behind the expedited courtship, an announcement was sent to the *Times* by Andrew, accompanied by one from Lord Cyril with the information on his daughter's courtship. It was unprecedented to announce a courtship in the papers, but given the reasons for the courtships, it was decided that it was a prudent step.

Both couples accepted the congratulations and hugs with humour and amusement. It was long understood what would happen for Elizabeth and Will, but Richard and Loretta were the welcome surprises to ensure that this was truly a newsworthy day. Elizabeth was pleased that her friend Retta would one day become her sister.

As Elaine watched, her heart tightened with a tinge of sadness that her beloved Reggie was not there to share in the joy with the rest of his family. This would have been the happiest of days for him. For Lizzy and Will to come to the point, yes, but for his second son to have such a wonderful future ahead would have eased the last of his worries.

"Does that mean we will have two brothers named William?" Tom Bennet asked.

"That is why I am Will, and your brother is William, Tom," Will grinned.

"You see, silly, and besides, Will is much taller than William," Kitty told her twin brother.

"He is not *that* much taller!" Tom did not enjoy being corrected by his sister.

It was decided that an impromptu celebratory dinner would be held at Matlock House. The previously planned dinners from Darcy House and Bennet House would be brought over to make sure there was sufficient repast for all.

~~~~~~~/~~~~~~~

The next morning as he broke his fast, the Earl of Granville was reading the *Times of London*. He was busy scheming as to how he would affect a compromise, if needed, to gain Lady Elizabeth's dowry of, he believed, greater than one hundred thousand pounds. Like many of his ilk, he over-calculated his ability to charm and was confident that he could direct her away from Darcy—after all, Darcy had no title. He was feeling smug until he reached the society pages and read the two announcements. He went into a rage which sent dishes flying from the table and crashing to the ground in a mess of food and broken china.

"This will not deter me!" he yelled at the wall. "I will have to compromise the chit, and the sooner, the better." He was sure they would be at some of the same balls, so he stalked to his study to see what invitations he had received. When he saw none, he yelled for his butler. When no one came, he remembered that he had let the man go as he could no longer afford the salary. He then summoned his housekeeper, one of the handful of servants that he retained.

"Yes, my Lord," the woman curtsied to the master.

"Where are all of my invitations?" he demanded.

"There are none, my Lord," came the answer, and he angrily waved her away.

He did not want to think about it, but it was not the first season that the invitations had dried up. His gaming and cavorting had become the fodder of many a scandal. His behaviour on its own would not have caused his being distanced by the Ton, but he had been involved in too many scandals, and word that he was not able to meet his financial obligations had not helped. He threw the snifter of brandy in his hand into the fire, causing a momentary flash of flames as the alcohol was consumed. He would have to pay attention to her habits and see if he could catch her out and about one day.

~~~~~~~/~~~~~~~

After the announcements had been published, both couples received a note of royal congratulations and an invitation for Lady Elizabeth and her suitor to Buckingham House. There were many other congratulatory notes received, even though some who had hoped to have the lady or her suitor as a daughter or son did so begrudgingly but would not do anything to run afoul of such a powerful family.

The fortune-hunting daughters and parents mourned the loss of the Honourable Mr. Richard Fitzwilliam as well once word of his true worth was discovered. For their male counterparts, the loss of Lady Loretta and her five and thirty thousand was not a happy occasion.

Elizabeth immersed herself in the season, enjoying the balls and soirées that she attended. The fact that Will was always with her made her enjoy that much more. Now that they were formally courting, Andrew had lifted his two-dance restriction, so the two routinely danced the first, supper, and final sets at each ball that they attended.

Richard and Loretta were revelling in their courtship, and they would dance the same three sets as Will and Lizzy at any ball they attended together. The more time they spent in one another's company, the more they both understood none was better suited to either of them. They talked about anything and everything and quickly discovered they had many interests in common, not the least of which was horses. Loretta did not just love to ride; she would join her father's hunt as well.

It looked like Wes was fated to be Richard's brother, just not how they would have preferred it to happen. As yet, he did not have a lady that excited his interest, but he did have to admit he had never held the depth of feeling Will Darcy had for Elizabeth, and in seeing their evident love, he finally accepted that what he felt was no more than an infatuation.

~~~~~~~/~~~~~~~

As it usually was, the visit to Buckingham House was a roaring success. The Queen seemed to never tire of hearing Lady Elizabeth Fitzwilliam play and sing. The royal stamp of approval was bestowed on the couple from her majesty. Once they married, the Darcys would become distant cousins to the royals, so the Queen's approval was positive, especially as it would become widely known in society that the possible match was looked on with a friendly eye by the royal family.

After the visit to the royals, Will and Elizabeth met Richard and Loretta, Georgiana, Kitty, Tom, and Alex at Gunter's. Originally Jane and Perry were to join them, but they had sent their regrets stating that Jane was somewhat fatigued.

"Did you enjoy your time with the royals, brother?" Georgiana asked.

"I will wager that our brother did not notice them as he would have been staring at Lizzy in that besotted manner of his," Alex ribbed his older brother.

"Sorry to disappoint you, *baby* brother, but I was aware of my surroundings. I cannot help that Lizzy has the voice of an angel that makes it impossible to concentrate on anything else when she sings," Will responded.

Elizabeth blushed at the praise from her suitor. She looked around when she felt the eyes of someone outside her party on her, but in seeing nothing amiss, she dismissed it as unimportant. Instead, she turned to her cousin Georgiana and younger sister to talk to them.

The Earl of Granville was sitting in the corner and scowling at them. As he was watching them, he lauded his luck at being at Gunter's at the same time by happenstance. He could see that it would be suicide to try anything inside of the establishment, as that damned Darcy never left her side. As he always ignored servants, he did not notice the huge footman looking at him as intently.

He was wise to refrain from any attempt where he was. He would not have been able to get close to her before he would have been dealt with, but he needed to marry her soon. He could not stave off the sale of his estate and townhouse for too many more days! He owed the bulk of his debts to a man they called *The Spaniard,* who would not hesitate to take his estate to satisfy his debts. He waited until the party he had been observing left Gunter's before he stood and paid his bill. Even though money was in short supply, he needed to keep up appearances.

Granville followed them back to Grosvenor Square and waited but waiting did nothing for him as he did not see his quarry again that day. He reluctantly made his way back to his shell of a townhouse on St. James Square.

CHAPTER 9

The Earl of Granville had seen Lady Elizabeth walk in Hyde Park, so he waited for her in the park on three consecutive days, but she had not been seen again. On the previous occasion, she had been with her suitor, and he thought he noticed some large footmen in the area. She also had a Great Dane with her, but from the white around the animal's snout, he surmised that it would not be a problem.

Time was running out. *The Spaniard* had given him an extension until the end of the current week to make a substantial payment on his over one hundred-thousand-pound debt; then, he would call in the debts and take his property. It was the first time in his life that Harry Smythe bemoaned the fact there was no entail on his estate or townhouse.

Granville left his townhouse that morning earlier that he liked to rise and headed toward Hyde Park. He sat on a bench away from the Grosvenor Square gate, where he had a clear view of those entering from the Square. He needed her to walk today. *The Spaniard* had told him, in no uncertain terms, that he had granted his final extension. He told himself it was not his fault he had had such a long run of bad luck, so it was not his fault that he needed to do what he was about to do.

~~~~~~~/~~~~~~~

It was a cold February day, but thankfully it was not snowing when Elizabeth left Matlock House for a ramble in Hyde Park. Two footmen walked ahead of her, Biggs and Johns behind her, and between them was Mrs. Annesley. Even Aggie had condescended to leave the warmth of the rug before the fire to accompany her mistress. Though she was nine when she was well rested, as she was as they left the house, a walk in the park was no trouble for her.

They entered the park with Aggie bounding about with more energy than Elizabeth had noted in a while. Elizabeth decided she would find a stick to throw for Aggie during her walk. As she walked, she was deep in thought about her Will, saddened that he had had to beg off the walk as he had a task to accomplish for his father that morning.

~~~~~~~/~~~~~~~

Lord Granville saw Lady Elizabeth as she entered the park. He could see at least two or three footmen with her, her companion, and her old dog. He saw the footmen but judged that there was enough distance for him to achieve his aim before they were able to reach him, and besides, as big as they were, they would be slow and lumbering.

Noting the path that she was taking; Granville made his way by a circuitous route where the path was close to a copse of trees. His plan was to *trip* and pull the lady down, tearing her dress in the process while making as much noise as he could to attract the maximum attention possible. She would have no choice then but to accept his offer to save her reputation. Her reputed dowry of over one hundred thousand was exactly what he needed to save himself and his properties from his creditors.

~~~~~~~/~~~~~~~

Will had been tasked to meet with his father's solicitors that morning, which was why he was not able to accompany Elizabeth on her ramble in Hyde Park as he would have preferred. He hoped that the documents that his father needed him to review at Mr. Reid's office would not keep him there too many hours as he was hoping to spend the afternoon with his Lizzy.

He had never enjoyed his time in society as he had since Elizabeth's coming out ball and all the subsequent events. He would never have believed that he, who had eschewed society as much as he had prior to the ball, would relish it now the way he did. He knew that the difference was Elizabeth, and without her, by his side, he would have been no keener for all the events that they had attended than he ever had.

Georgiana had always loved him, but now that he was on the cusp of proposing to Lizzy and making the two young ladies sisters, his sister showed him adoration akin to hero-worship. It seemed that Elizabeth had that effect on those around her.

His parents were no less pleased than Georgiana; they just did not show it in the boisterous manner she did. Alex was the only one who seemed indifferent. He loved his cousin, but whether she was cousin or sister did not seem to impact his life.

"Mr. Darcy, welcome," Mr. Reid welcomed his client's son. "If you will follow me to the reading room, the documents are ready for you."

"Thank you, Mr. Reid." Will followed the man to the designated room, and thankfully it was not a big stack of documents —only about ten pages in total. No matter how much he wanted to be with Elizabeth, he would read the pages with care. This was his duty, and it was not in his nature to shirk any duty he had to perform.

~~~~~~~/~~~~~~~

Richard made his way to Jersey House to call on Loretta. It had been a few weeks of courtship, and his tender feelings had progressed to love. He suspected it was the same for Loretta, but he did not want to rush in headlong like it was a cavalry charge. He was hoping his lady would agree to take a curricle ride with him through Hyde Park.

The butler showed him in where the four members of the De Melville family were ensconced in a morning parlour. "Good morning, Richard," Lord Cyril welcomed him.

"Good morning all," Richard said, but his gaze was fixed on Loretta. "I would like to invite Loretta to ride with me through the park," he requested.

"Is there room for her companion in the vehicle?" her father asked.

"Unfortunately not, my Lord, it is a curricle that only seats two with ease," Richard explained.

"I will ride my horse and accompany them," Wes volunteered.

"As will Loretta's companion and a groom," Lord Cyril decided.

So it was that a half-hour later, Loretta was bundled up next to Richard in the curricle, and the three riders mounted and were ready to depart. They started toward the park with Wes on the side of the vehicle where Richard was sitting and the other two following not far behind.

"You are not too cold, are you, Reta?" Richard asked. The last thing he wanted was for her to have an experience she did not enjoy.

"I am well, Richard; besides the warming bricks, I have many layers of clothing to keep me warm, and how can I feel cold when I am seated next to you?" A blush spread across her cheeks as she said the last softly.

They entered the park from the west and took a route that would lead them to the Grosvenor Square gate.

~~~~~~~~/~~~~~~~~

Granville was pleased; the dog had taken off chasing a rabbit or some such; the companion was a little behind his intended victim, and the huge footmen were behind her. A few more minutes and his money issues would be over. He hid next to a birch tree trunk that was just off the path.

Elizabeth was lost in thoughts of the man that she loved when she heard a noise to her right. She saw an unknown man barrelling towards her. Both Biggs and Johns saw the man lunging at their charge and broke into a run. For Elizabeth, time seemed to stand still as the man was about to reach her, and from the looks of things, he meant to grab her dress. She turned to start to run, knowing that it would be futile as he was so close to her. The two footmen were still a few feet away and watched helplessly as the man was inches from Lady Elizabeth.

Just as his fingers touched Lady Elizabeth's dress, he was sent flying back. Before he knew what had happened, he was staring into the eyes of a menacingly growling dog that was drooling all over his face. He felt an inordinate amount of pain on his chest where the beast had jumped on him and forced him to the ground with its front paws. Rather than not being a factor as he had calculated, Lady Elizabeth's dog had thwarted him.

Just when things could not get worse, the dog moved aside, and he was lifted off the ground and suspended in the air like a ragdoll. "Good girl, Aggie," Elizabeth petted her dog, who looked much younger than her years in that moment and was waging her tail furiously. Just then, several horses came to a sudden stop, and Richard, Wes, and Retta appeared before Elizabeth. Richard could see that his sister was unharmed, and then he saw the blackguard, Granville.

The man used to be a good friend of his and Andrew's until he came into his inheritance at one and twenty when his parents were killed in an accident. He had changed overnight to become the dishonourable man that he was today, causing the bonds of friendship to be broken by the Fitzwilliam brothers, who would not associate with one such as he.

"Why is Granville hanging about?" Richard asked. He then indicated Biggs should allow the man to stand on his own two feet.

"I was minding my own business when that brute of a dog attacked me for no reason," Granville blustered. "If that was not bad enough, I was set upon by your pet giant here. I should call the runners and have the dog put down and the man arrested for accosting a peer of the realm."

"You lie!" Elizabeth practically yelled from where she stood next to Retta. "He tried to attack me; he was about to grab my gown when Aggie saved me. He was seen by our men and Mrs. Annesley as well," she reported with anger. "I will wager the stupid man was trying to compromise me!"

"That is not what happened; no one will believe this chit over me!" Granville tried to assert, but before he could say another word, and after a nod from Richard, one of the footmen landed a massive fist in the man's stomach. The Earl was left in more pain than when the dog felled him while he gasped for breath.

"I have heard you were deep in debt, and to *The Spaniard* no less, Granville. That man will not forgive a debt, especially one of over one hundred thousand. I am confused; did you think that man would accept half of what you owe him?" Richard asked.

"Half! I heard that she…" Another blow landed.

"Lady Elizbeth to you," Johns hissed after he withdrew his fist.

"I was told *Lady Elizbeth's* dowry was over one hundred thousand." Granville dropped all pretence.

"Unlike you, I care about others and have donated half of my dowry to charity. Even if you had succeeded, I would never have married you," Elizabeth informed the shocked man, her voice dripping in heavy disdain.

"Firstly, her dowry would only be released if both my brother and her birth father approved of the man *prior* to his proposing. Secondly, if you had compromised her, you would have done my cousin Darcy and my sister a favour; they would have married right away. You would be in the same position, about to lose your family homes to a debt collector. Notwithstanding that, you will answer to the law for attempting to assault my sister, who you may remember is a favourite of the King and Queen." Richard demolished weeks of Granville's delusional plans in but minutes. "Wes, will you accompany two of the footmen to the runners to deposit that with them?" he pointed at Granville with derision.

"With pleasure. It will be an honour to assist in ridding society of the cancer that is Granville," Wes agreed cheerfully. One of the two footmen who had walked ahead of Lady Elizabeth removed a length of rope from the curricle. Granville was led away, head down, trussed up like a common criminal, while the rest moved in the direction of Matlock House.

~~~~~~~~/~~~~~~~~

"I did not expect you back from your walk so soon, Lizzy," her mother exclaimed as her daughter walked into the drawing room accompanied by her son, his lady, and Aggie, who was looking most pleased with herself.

"My walk was cut short by an unscrupulous earl who believed my dowry was over one hundred thousand—the amount he needed to satisfy his creditors," Elizabeth informed her mother, Andrew, and Marie.

"Granville! I will kill the basta…Sorry ladies, I should have regulated my words, but I will kill him! What did he do to you, Lizzy?" a seething Andrew asked, not understanding why his brother and sister looked so complacent.

"He never laid a hand on my person, brother; you can relax. For that, we have our heroine Aggie to thank. She had taken off chasing a small animal, but she must have been close enough to perceive the man was a threat because as he was about to grab my dress, Aggie came flying out of nowhere, and the man was on his back with my dog growling in his face. If he had tried anything further to harm me, he would have discovered just how powerful her jaws are," Elizabeth explained, as she scratched Aggie behind the ears.

"Good girl, Aggie!" Elaine exclaimed, "Your father knew she would always protect Lizzy just as she did today." Aggie revelled in all the attention and petting that she received.

"She will have a steak for dinner," Marie commanded.

"What of Granville?" Andrew asked; his pique had calmed once he knew his sister was unharmed.

"On his way to the runners, escorted by my brother," Loretta stated.

"*The Spaniard* will own his properties within days," Andrew opined. "That man cares nothing for rank; if you owe you pay, or he claims your collateral. Gambling is a fool's game."

"He frittered away generations of accumulated wealth in the matter of a few years, and then he looked to our Lizzy to save him. The man we knew at Cambridge is long dead. He is lucky that he did not manage to lay a hand on Lizzy. I was ready to lay into him and would have had even his finger touched our sister," Richard told the group. Granville would have had a lot more than his dignity hurt if Richard had been required to act.

"Will is going to want to gallop to the gaol and call the man out when he finds out," Andrew verbalised what any who knew Will was thinking.

"Why would I want to do that?" came from the doorway. "Did something happen to Lizzy?" Will asked, feeling his fury mount at the possibility until he saw she was well and smiling at him.

The morning's adventure was explained to him, and like Andrew had stated, Will did want to jump onto Zeus and find the man and rip him end from end. "Will, I am completely well," Elizabeth assured him.

"What a good dog you are, Aggie," Will lavished her with praise and kneeled down and scratched her chest when she rolled onto her back, her hind leg kicking the air as she was scratched in the place she loved best.

"If there is even a whiff of scandal that Lizzy was compromised, then I will hie to the Archbishop's offices, acquire a special licence, and we will marry as soon as may be!" Will stated firmly.

"In that event, which I doubt will happen, then yes, that will be an acceptable solution, as long as Lizzy is agreeable to it," Andrew allowed.

"If need be, and you and Father Bennet give your consent, I will marry Will earlier than planned. In that respect, Granville would end up doing me a favour," Elizabeth said as she looked at Will lovingly.

"Yes, he would be very useful in that respect," Will winked at her.

"There was no one near to witness his cowardly attempt other than us, Wes, and our employees, so *if* the attempted attack is spoken of when Granville is tried, we will be able to control the narrative. It has long been that no one in the Ton gives credence to anything that waste of a man says," Richard reminded everyone. "I know in this case that you two," he looked at his sister and cousin, "would prefer there was a reason to advance the date of your marriage, but I am confident you will be disappointed."

As they talked about the possibility, or lack thereof, of an early wedding, Wes De Melville entered the drawing room. "Granville is gone," he said simply.

"How?" Will, Andrew, and Richard asked simultaneously.

"One of the footmen was leading him by the rope that secured him. When we were close to Bow Street, a carriage was approaching at speed. Granville ran into the footman, causing him to drop the rope, and took the coward's way out by throwing himself under the carriage wheels. The driver attempted to halt the team, but it was too late. By the time we reached him, he was no more," Wes related.

"No early wedding, Lizzy," her mother said with evidently false sadness, thereby lightening the news. She knew it was only months away, but that was better than a few days.

"I wager he could not live with the shame of losing his family's legacy. A small mercy is he had no blood relatives alive. As he never married and sired an heir, the Granville line is at an end and shall only be remembered for the ignominy of his actions, and Lizzy's name will never be aligned with him. If anyone asks, we will let it be known that he attempted to rob a gentleman and was being arrested when he took the cowardly option," Andrew stated.

All present agreed that what Andrew said made sense. There would be no one to mourn the last Earl of Granville. When London woke up to the news of his death the next morning, *The Spaniard* filed the paperwork to take possession of the man's property. Within days the estate and townhouse were on the market as *The Spaniard* wanted cash, not property. There were none in society who cared enough about Granville to enquire about the circumstances of his final downfall, so the story about an attempted robbery was not needed. To Elizabeth and Will's chagrin, there was no reason to marry right away.

~~~~~~~/~~~~~~~

At dinner that night at Bennet House, the Bennets and Darcys were informed of the day's events, and then the name Granville was never mentioned again. Preparations were made for Elizabeth's and Georgiana's birthday and for the betrothal all knew would happen as soon as Will walked to Matlock House the morning of the fifth of March.

CHAPTER 10

March fifth, 1799

Elizabeth had a hard time falling asleep the previous night. In fact, by the time she finally gave in to her tiredness, it was after midnight. She was eighteen, and it was the day that she would get one of her wishes granted, to become betrothed to Will. Like a good number of nights when alone in her bed, Elizabeth daydreamed of Will, of her being with him like she had often thought about over the last months especially.

As she imagined being kissed by him, much more thoroughly than the one kiss they had shared the day she accepted his offer of courtship, Elizabeth felt warm all over. She knew that there was more than just kissing, but she was not educated beyond the cold, clinical descriptions she had read in some books. Those descriptions did not excite her passions like thoughts of Will did, but clinical had its uses. She still felt like a wanton when she gave in to her desire to relieve the pressure, imagining it was him that was touching her so intimately. When she finally felt the release, and after she calmed down, she succumbed to her exhaustion and fell asleep.

~~~~~~~/~~~~~~~

Across the square, Will was preparing for the biggest day of his life so far. He patted his waistcoat pocket where his late grandmother Darcy's ring was in the velvet-covered ring box. His mother had chosen the ring her late mother wore, and until his father retrieved the ring from the vault, it had not been worn since his grandmother's time. As his man Carstens completed his work on the cravat, Will thought back to the conversation he had had with Uncle Thomas the day before.

Will had walked across to Bennet House in the morning, and when the butler opened the door, Will requested to see the master. Knowing that his master was waiting for the young man in his study, the butler announced him to Bennet and withdrew, closing the door behind him.

"Good morning, Will, would you like some coffee?" Bennet offered as he sat.

"No, thank you, Mr. Bennet; I had some with my parents before I left Darcy House."

"So formal, Will. Have I not been Uncle Thomas for a while now?" Bennet asked dryly.

"You have, but I am here to ask the most important of questions, so I felt that formality is appropriate," Will explained.

"The floor is yours." Bennet sat back. Will knew that Uncle Thomas was aware of his purpose, but he could see that the older man would not make things too easy for him and respected that. He wanted to go through the process of asking, and an edge of uncertainty reassured him that while Lizzy was his alone, he had to be worthy of her in all ways.

"My purpose today is to request the honour of your daughter Elizabeth's hand in marriage. If you have no objection, I have Andrew's leave to ask her to become my betrothed today," Will's words were a steady stream, but when he had stated his request, he took a long, deep breath and held it as he waited for Bennet's reply.

"It would be easy to toy with you and ask you inane questions like do you love her, can you support her, or will you be good to her, but I know the answers to those questions, so I only have one. Why Lizzy? Why do you want to marry her and not someone else?" Uncle Thomas asked.

As was his wont when considering a weighty issue, Will took his time to answer. "It is because I cannot imagine my life without her in it, and I do not mean as a cousin. She challenges me, never blindly agrees with what I say like so many women looking to marry in the Ton do, and never has an issue correcting me.

"Some would tell me that it is not a good idea to marry one who is

far more intelligent than you, but her intelligence is one of the things that has always drawn me to her. I assume you know the story of when she was about seven, and I became infatuated with her mind and the mess I made of things at the time?" Uncle Thomas nodded, allowing that he had heard the infamous story. "Her mind was the first thing to captivated me; it was not until she was around fifteen that I was captivated by the rest of her.

"Elizabeth had always been one of, if not the, most beautiful woman in any room, but as she got older, her beauty has only increased for me. She is outwardly exquisite, but who she is inside is what is most important to me. She always puts other's needs ahead of her own and is one of the most caring and compassionate people that I know. In short, she is the only woman I could ever marry. If she were to refuse me, I would not marry at all.

"Knowing that Elizabeth wants to marry me as much as I want to marry her means unless you refuse me, I will marry her," Will concluded the speech.

"If I were to refuse you, which I have no intention of, I would lose my daughter again, and there is nothing that will induce me to be the cause of that. I may be older, but I am not blind; I see how she adores you and how besotted you are. I could not have parted with her again to a man less worthy. Yes, Will, you have my hearty consent and blessing. I know you will make her happy," Uncle Thomas concluded.

Finally, the day was here. Will was so happy he almost floated down the grand stairs. His parents were in the breakfast parlour —his father with a steaming mug of coffee while his mother sipped her tea. "Where are you off to so early, Will?" his mother teased him.

"Yes, son, sit and relax. I cannot imagine why you would want to rush out at such an early hour," George followed his wife.

"I have waited longer than I would have liked to for this day to arrive, so before some other buffoon gets it in his head to try and compromise my love, I think it is time to walk to Matlock House," Will informed his parents.

"I assume you will bring my future daughter to receive our well wishes after you are betrothed, will you not, Will?" Anne asked.

"It may be after Bennet House, but yes, mother, we will be here this morning, and when we arrive, Lizzy will be wearing Grandmama Darcy's ring." Will waited impatiently while Killion helped him into his outerwear, then he bounded down the stairs that led to the square and his destiny awaiting him at Matlock House.

~~~~~~~/~~~~~~~

The five Fitzwilliams were about to conclude breaking their fasts when Will was announced. The four older family members had to fight breaking into laughter at seeing Elizabeth wanting to jump out of her chair, her good manners only just checking her from doing so.

"Welcome, Will," Andrew intoned, "are you here to join us in breaking our fasts? I am afraid as we are almost finished, so you may have to return tomorrow," he ribbed his cousin.

"**Andrew**!" Elizabeth shouted.

"Yes, Sprite?" Andrew asked innocently.

"You know very well why Will is here this morning!" Elizabeth huffed.

"To wish you a happy birthday," Richard pilled on. "He could have waited until the party this evening; there was no need for him to run across the Square before calling hours."

"Richard Fitzwilliam, you are *not* funny," Elizabeth scowled at her bothers.

"If you two are done making sport, mayhap you will allow Will to tell us why he is here," Elaine looked at both her sons, who were sporting huge grins, happy that they were able to discompose Will and Lizzy at the same time.

"Thank you, Aunt; I am here to request a private interview with Elizabeth," Will stated, relieved to finally be able to say the words. It had seemed like forever, but, on some level, he had to admit he would have been disappointed had his cousins not teased him, which would be a sign of change in their regard.

"Why would you need…" Richard started to say, stopping when he received a sharp, unladylike kick on his shin from his sister, who gave him a warning look. He raised his hands in surrender.

"My little Reggie behaves better than you two sometimes, and he is not yet two!" Marie rolled her eyes at the antics of her husband and brother.

"I assume that you spoke to Uncle Thomas?" Andrew asked, and Will nodded. "You may use the small parlour. I will give you ten minutes, and the door will remain partially open with Mrs. Annesley sitting outside," he stipulated.

Elizabeth jumped out of her seat like she had been shot out of a cannon, which resulted in a guffaw from the direction of her brothers and some soft tittering from ladies at the table--she cared not a whit. "It seems that there is something that you have to say that our Lizzy wishes to hear," Marie smiled sweetly, her eyes as knowing as everyone else and well-remembered her own excitement.

Will closed the door to the parlour three-quarters of the way once Mrs. Annesley was comfortable in her chair, which faced the door from the hall. "May I just say yes so we can proceed to the part where you kiss me?" she asked hopefully.

"We will get there soon enough, but I do want to ask properly if that is all the same with you, Lizzy." He chuckled, and she nodded, sighing in happiness when he went down on one knee and took her hands in his. "I never believed I had the capacity to love anyone the way I love you. You are my everything, Elizabeth Rose Bennet Fitzwilliam. It has been a long time since I have known that you are the only woman that I could ever be happy with as my wife.

"I love you, Lizzy, and will spend the rest of my life dedicated to your felicity. I could not respect you more, your intelligence, charity, compassion, and your capacity to laugh. Will you do me the greatest honour of my life and accept my hand. Please marry me, Lizzy."

"Oh, Will, I love you too and have loved you for a long time as a woman loves a man. I love you in infinite ways and could never marry anyone but you, so it seems that we were formed for one another. You are my soulmate, Will, so I will repeat what I said before you asked, yes, yes, I will marry you. You have made me the happiest of women." She nodded, wiping aside her tears of joy as she accepted the man she loved beyond reason.

Will stood, then withdrew the box with his grandmother's ring from his waistcoat. He took her left hand and slid the diamond, emerald, and gold ring onto her fourth finger. "It is perfect, Will," Elizabeth gushed as she looked at the ring that fits as if it had been made for her.

Will then drew Elizabeth to him. Like their first kiss, their lips brushed, but this time he did not stop. She sighed her acquiescence as she wound her arms around his neck, so he was not able to escape, although he had no thought to try. The next kiss was deeper as they tasted each other, and soon she felt his tongue teasing her lips, and Elizabeth opened them instinctively.

Their tongues met in an explosion of passion as they pressed their bodies against one another, so there was no daylight between them. He felt her pert breasts against his chest, and she felt evidence of his arousal against her belly. As the ten-minute time limit approached, they heard Lizzy's companion clear her throat, and the two pulled apart reluctantly.

As they stood forehead to forehead with almost a foot between them as they soaked in the sight of each other, he could not miss the points that Elizabeth's nipples were making in her gown, and she did not miss the large bulge in his breeches. As both took deep breaths, the visible signs of their arousal receded, then they put themselves to rights and exited the parlour, trying and failing to look as passive as could be.

"The family awaits you in the drawing room, Lady Elizabeth and Mr. Darcy," Mrs. Annesley informed them, trying, and failing to hide a smile.

"May I meet with you, Andrew?" Will requested on entering the drawing room.

"There is no need to, Will," Andrew replied. Just as the newly betrothed couple was about to make their displeasure known, he continued, "You already have both my permission and my blessing, and I assume that you do not want to ask me to lengthen the three-month betrothal period. So given that, do you still require an interview?"

"No, he does not!" Elizabeth stated emphatically.

"Look at that, Will, you are not even married yet, and she is making decisions for you," Richard teased them both.

"I know that you two will be extremely happy together," Elaine said as she drew her daughter into a hug. She was followed by Andrew and Richard, and lastly, Marie hugged her sister-in-law.

"What an exquisite ring, Lizzy," Marie proclaimed as she lifted Elizabeth's left hand. While she was admiring the ring, Elaine was kissing her soon-to-be son's cheek.

"What should I call you from now on, Aunt Elaine?" Will asked after she had kissed him.

"Mother Elaine will do as Marie calls me. Never hurt her, Fitzwilliam!" she reminded him.

"Never again, Mother Elaine. It will be my life's work," he swore.

"See that it is, soon-to-be brother, or you will have me to answer to," Richard warned as he shook Will's hand.

"What he said," Andrew added as he shook the hand that Richard had let go.

"Ignore my husband and brother," Marie stated as she kissed Will's cheek. "They are full of bluster, and they may not admit it yet, but they know there is no one who will be a better husband for Lizzy in the known world. Welcome as my soon-to-be brother. I just realised, I will now have more brothers and sisters than I ever dreamed I would." Marie just realised that she already was sister to all the Bennet children, and now she would be sister to Georgiana and Alex as well, and she could not forget to count her Ashby siblings.

After the butler handed out flutes of champagne, a toast was given to the newly betrothed couple. "Have you two decided on a date yet?" Andrew asked.

"Based on your three-month stipulation, we could marry on

the fifth day of June. Do you agree, Lizzy?" Will asked.

"That would be a fine day to marry, but do you mind waiting just a little more than a fortnight, Will?" Elizabeth asked hopefully.

"Of course, you want to be married on the twentieth of June, the day that your brothers discovered you in Sherwood and brought you home to your mother and father," Will said. "I think that will be a perfect day to marry from Snowhaven."

"That is the perfect date," Elaine said as a few tears escaped her eyes as she thought about how much her beloved Reggie would have loved walking his daughter down the aisle to give her to Will.

~~~~~~~/~~~~~~~

Just before half-past ten, the newly betrothed couple was shown into the family sitting room at Bennet House. Jane, Perry, and Lady Rose were present in anticipation of the glad tidings. As soon as Elizabeth entered the room, all of the ladies spied her ring and jumped up to congratulate the couple.

Jane had felt the quickening the previous morning but was waiting until the next day, not wanting to detract from her sister's news. "You will be very happy, Lizzy," Jane promised as she hugged her sister tightly.

"I am so happy, Jane; how can one person deserve so much happiness?" Elizabeth gushed.

"With your goodness, you deserve it all and more," Jane said softly in Elizabeth's ear.

Next, she was hugged by Mother Bennet, Kitty, Perry, and Tom. That left Father Bennet, who enfolded her in a hug. "You will be a very happy woman, Lizzy," he told her, "I pity anyone who tries to take advantage of either of you; it is a mistake they will make but one time."

"Thank you, Father Bennet. On the day I marry, will you share the duties of walking me down the aisle with Andrew?" she requested.

"It will be my greatest honour to do so if Andrew agrees," Bennet responded.

"He will agree," Elizabeth stated with certainty as she arched her eyebrow.

Another toast was given and humbly accepted by the betrothed couple, and a second toast was given for Elizabeth's birthday.

~~~~~~~/~~~~~~~

On entering the music room at Darcy House, and before a word could be uttered, Georgiana flew into Elizabeth's arms. "Happy birthday, Sister," she gushed.

"Happy birthday to you too, my soon-to-be sister," Elizabeth responded as she hugged her cousin, friend, and soon-to-be sister Gigi. "We will celebrate our birthdays later this evening."

"Who cares about a birthday when you are betrothed to Will!" Georgiana exclaimed.

"We are very happy to welcome you as a daughter," George gave his niece a hug.

"Lizzy will be my cousin and my sister?" Alex asked.

"Yes, son," Anne replied and then kissed her new daughter's cheeks. "I could not have asked for a better daughter-in-law, Lizzy. Do you have a date for the wedding?"

When the date was shared, both George and Anne Darcy nodded, Anne's eyes misty at the memory of the day she had been notified of Elizabeth being found. "When will Andrew have the announcement placed in the papers?" George asked.

"He will send it to them this morning, so it should be in tomorrow's editions," Will informed his father.

"Will it be acceptable if I call you Mother Anne and Father George from now on? Will is going to call Mama Mother Elaine." Both of her parents-in-law-to-be agreed.

"I would be fine with your using them from today forward, Lizzy. We have long known you would be our daughter one day, though those who can marry very young never learn who they are intended to be until much later in life. Glad you two are finally getting around to it, though." George grinned when Lizzy and Will stared at him in surprise because to them; it had felt like an eternity; it had never occurred to them that it had been done this way to give them the best chance at success.

"So are we." Lizzy smiled at him, the immense shift of her thoughts taking only a second and the wisdom of those who loved them catching her anew.

After more talk of the upcoming union, Will walked Elizabeth back to Matlock House to rest so that she would be refreshed for the celebratory birthday and betrothal dinner, which would be held at the Fitzwilliams' house that evening. Along with the Darcys, Bennets, and Rhys-Davies, the Gardiners, Phillips, Ashbys, and De Melvilles were invited to share their celebration.

As can be expected, the dinner was a much-enjoyed celebration, and Georgiana was proven correct—they were acknowledged and wishes given, but little attention was paid to the birthdays when there was a betrothal to celebrate.

The next morning the Ton awoke to their papers that proclaimed another extremely eligible bachelor was no longer available to their daughters. There was much remonstrating in private, but none would dare say a word against the match in public.

CHAPTER 11

Richard had no more doubt. He was in love with Lady Loretta De Melville and was fairly sure his feelings were returned. The family was to decamp to the north in a fortnight, and he did not want to have Loretta's family leave London for their estate, Broadhurst in Essex, before he had asked her the most important of questions.

He was aware they would be in Derbyshire in June for Lizzy and Will's wedding, but he could not wait that long before offering her his hand in marriage. It was a cool spring day when Richard dismounted his horse and handed the reins to the waiting groom in front of Jersey House. He was admitted by the butler and requested to see Lord Cyril.

"Sit, Richard," Lord Cyril indicated to a chair in front of his desk after the butler closed the door.

"Good morning, your Lordship; I am here to request a private interview with your daughter," Richard asked, not one for small talk when there was a task to accomplish as crucial as the one before him this day.

"I assume it is to request Loretta's hand in marriage." Lord Cyril asked for Richard was not the only one who was candid.

"It is, my Lord." Richard agreed with a quick nod.

"I will not insult your intelligence to ask about your situation again, Richard. I know you are more than able to afford a wife, so you have my permission to see Loretta in private. Ten minutes; the door will be open partway and remember there are large footmen in the hall. Wait here. I will ask Loretta to join you." The Earl rose and left to find his daughter.

"Papa said you wanted an audience with me, Richard. Why so formally today? You call on me practically every day...unless you have a particular reason to see me today," Loretta surmised when she saw him stand tall, relieved that Richard was finally ready to get to the point.

"It is for a very special reason that I requested to see you alone, Loretta," Richard agreed. As he dropped to one knee, he took her left hand in his right. "Loretta Hazel De Melville, I love you; I am in love with you and do not want another day, another minute, to pass without declaring my undying love for you. Will you do me the great honour of accepting my hand in marriage?" Richard held his breath as he waited for her response.

"I have been dreaming of this day for some time, Richard. It is my heart's fondest desire to marry you as I love you deeply. Yes, Richard, I most certainly will be your wife, for it is a position I have long hoped to fill," Loretta said with pleasure.

Richard slid a simple gold ring with a large, empire-cut centre diamond with smaller ones to either side of her finger. He had had the ring made for her, declining both his brother and mother's offer to take one from them. He wanted to give her something new, something that no one had ever worn before, something that he had had a hand in making perfect for her.

He stood and saw the permission in her eyes to kiss her, something both had been wanting for months, but there had been no chance. Their first kiss was anything but chaste as they allowed their mutual desire to rule. Loretta's hands snaked around his waist as his brushed one of her breasts on the way to cup her cheek.

Loretta let out a gasp of pleasure, taking his hand in hers and pressing it to the side of her breast in hope for him to do it again and sighing in relief when the feathered touch of his thumb explored her. She could not wait for more, but she knew that standing in her father's study with the partially open door was neither the time nor place. All too soon, they parted, and it was not a full minute before there was a warning knock on the door that allowed them just enough time to put themselves to rights.

The Earl and Countess walked in. The Countess looked amused as she spied her daughter's swollen lips. "I assume that you accepted him, Loretta, by the ring on your left hand?" her father asked, trying not to see the very things his wife was enjoying the seeing off.

"Yes, Papa, I most certainly did!" Loretta exclaimed.

"I request your consent and blessing to marry your daughter, Lord Cyril and Lady Sarah," Richard asked. He knew it was unnecessary to ask Loretta's mother, but he felt it was a mark of respect to her as she was present, and it was her humour and example Loretta followed closest which had caught his attention.

"Welcome to the family, son. You have our consent and our heartfelt blessing." Lord Cyril extended his hand to Richard.

"Have you discussed a date?" Lady Sarah asked after hugging and congratulating her daughter.

"We have not, Mama," Loretta answered.

"Do you have a minimum requirement for the betrothal, Lord Cyril?" Richard inquired.

"I think we can dispense with the Lord, and you shall call me Father Cyril. My minimum is two months," Lord Cyril replied, not missing his daughter's disappointment. "You will find that two months will pass very fast, and besides, your mother would have me hung, drawn, and quartered if I did not allow her time enough to organise the wedding of her only daughter."

"We will marry from Broadhurst unless you object, Richard," Loretta looked at her newly minted fiancé expectantly.

"You will hear no objection from me. I do have one suggestion, though. As Will and Lizzy will marry on the twentieth of June, would you mind if we wait until the beginning of August to make sure that my sister and new brother will be able to attend our nuptials?" Richard requested hopefully.

"As much as I would like to marry sooner, I too would like them at our wedding, so yes, Richard, I have no objection to early August," Loretta responded lovingly.

"The first day of August is a Thursday, if that is acceptable to both of you," Lady Sarah said as she consulted a calendar in her husband's study and the newly betrothed couple agreed to the date.

"If I have your permission, Father Cyril, Mother Sarah, would it be possible for Loretta to accompany me to Matlock House to share the good tidings with my family?" Richard requested.

"She may, but she will be with my wife and me in the carriage, so we can be there as well when you share your good news with your family." Lord Cyril chuckled. He only had one daughter, and so in seeing her pleasure, he did not intend to miss sharing the happiness of Elaine's as she would with himself and Sarah had the roles been reversed.

~~~~~~~/~~~~~~~

Andrew and Marie departed Town at the end of April so that Marie would be back at Snowhaven well before her confinement. Richard was left responsible for Matlock House, his mother, and his sister. As the Bennets and Darcys were also in Town, there was no shortage of men for protection when needed.

Elizabeth was sitting next to Will as their mothers were discussing the impending wedding. There would be an engagement ball at Pemberley on the Friday prior to the wedding; it was now less than a sennight to the day, and Will and Lizzy wished it already passed. The invitations had been sent, and answers received, to which there had been almost no negative replies. The Duchess of Kent had replied for their Majesties and family with regrets as the wedding was so far out of London.

Conversation stopped as Richard led Loretta into the drawing room, holding her hand, and her beaming parents followed behind the couple. Elizabeth did not miss the ring on her friend's, and evidently soon to be sister's, finger. She was about to jump up and hug her friend and her brother but knowing that her brother was about to make an announcement, she remained seated.

"It is with the greatest of pleasure that I can announce that Loretta accepted my hand in marriage," Richard grinned as he shared his news. After receiving a congratulatory hug from his mother, Richard opened his arms to receive his younger sister.

"Oh, I knew how it would be. You and Retta are perfect for each other, Itch. I could not be happier to gain my friend as my newest sister. If wealth were measured in family, then we would be the wealthiest family in the kingdom," Elizabeth told her brother as she kissed his cheek.

"Well, well," Will clapped Richard on the back, "I never thought you would allow yourself to be leg shackled."

"You have no room to talk, Will. You will be entering that state before me," Richard returned his cousin's good-natured ribbing.

Richard and Loretta shared the date and location of their wedding with the family. "Will we have completed our wedding trip by then, Will?" Elizabeth asked in concern as she did not want to miss the wedding.

"We will return about a sennight before the first day of August, so we will be in attendance," he reassured Elizabeth. "In fact, rather than returning to Pemberley, we will travel directly to Broadhurst if that is acceptable to the De Melvilles."

"You know that you need not ask. You will be more than welcome," Lady Sarah shook her head at their children, amused at the request.

After informing the Bennets of the good news, Richard and Loretta returned to Matlock House. The De Melville's accepted an invitation to stay for one of the family's impromptu dinners. Cook just shook her head good-naturedly and sent a boy over to Darcy House to coordinate with her now extended staff as hers was theirs.

~~~~~~~/~~~~~~~

As scheduled, while the Fitzwilliams were still in Town, the Darcys and the extended Bennet family departed London for Derbyshire. The Bennets, Phillipses, and Gardiners were to be hosted at Pemberley. The official reason being that with Marie entering her confinement and a wedding to be held at Snowhaven, it would be easier for the three families to stay at the Darcys' estate.

On the first day of travel, Elizabeth was staring out of the window at her ever more handsome betrothed as she recalled the conversation that they had with Father George a few days before their departure from London.

Elizabeth and Will had been asked to meet with his father in the master's study at Darcy House.

"Once you two are married, would you not prefer your own home rather than a suite of rooms at Pemberley?" Father George had asked.

"Will and I have discussed this, Father George, and we will be happy at Pemberley with you, Mother Anne, and our brother and sister," Elizabeth responded.

"That was not the question that I asked you. The question is what you would prefer, not what you would be happy with," Father George insisted.

"What are you thinking, Father? I know you would not ask such a question unless you had something in mind," Will asked, smiling at his father's quick grin.

"You have the right of it, Will. You have visited our estate Rivington in Cheshire on numerous occasions, have you not?" he asked.

"Yes, father, I have. Are you suggesting we should live at your second estate?" Will asked.

"Not at my *second estate, but at* yours. *Your mother and I are gifting you Rivington for your wedding. Before you object, one day, when God calls me to Him, it will be yours anyway. You will be welcome at Pemberley any time, but this way, you two will start your married life in your own home," Father George explained.*

"That is so much!" Elizabeth had exclaimed, "That estate clears over eight thousand a year."

"When, please God, you two have your own children, you will see that this not too much. Unless you tell me you prefer not to live in your own home, it is done." He sat back to wait.

After a brief discussion, Will and Elizabeth gratefully accepted. As the estate was just over the western border of Derbyshire, less than twenty miles from Pemberley and not more than fifteen from Snowhaven, it would not make it too far away to see their family when they desired to, as had been their plan after their marriage.

A day later, when sharing their good fortune with Jane and Perry, the latter had pointed out that as Longfield Meadows was in the West Riding part of Yorkshire, it was just over thirty miles, making Rivington's location that much more attractive.

Elizabeth was brought out of her reverie when she heard Aggie snore. As it was just her mother and herself in the carriage, Aggie was lying on the floor between them.

Richard was not happy that he would be parted from his betrothed, but he consoled himself with the knowledge Loretta would be arriving in Derbyshire in less than a fortnight. Her family was being hosted at Pemberley, and that was no obstacle given the short distance between Brookfield and Pemberley. He was very much looking forward to showing Loretta and her family her future home.

Thomas Bennet had no complaint that he would be *forced* to be at Pemberley and near the library that he occasionally saw in his dreams. On the third day of travel, the caravan of coaches came to a halt at Snowhaven.

The footmen who opened the doors all seemed to be smiling; their questions were answered when Andrew stood in the doorway of the manor house with a little bundle swaddled in pink in his arms. If the baby's grandmother had been younger, she would have run, propriety be damned, but befitting her age, she walked gracefully at the fastest pace she was able to where her beaming son was standing. No one thought of usurping the second-time grandmother's right to see her new grandchild first, though they were all anxious to meet her.

"Welcome home, Mama; I present to you Tiffany Rose Fitzwilliam; she was born on the two and twentieth when you were already more than halfway home. By the time a messenger found you, you would have been hours away from Snowhaven anyway," Andrew soothed his mother's frown when she glared at him for not having informed her.

"How is my daughter?" his mother asked. By now, everyone was converging on Andrew, so he made the wise decision to retreat to the nearest drawing room where little Tiffany's nursemaid was waiting.

"Marie is doing as well as the doctor and midwife have seen anyone do after more than twelve hours of labour. She is expected to make a full recovery and should be well enough to see people on the morrow." Andrew relayed as his family crowded around him to get a glimpse at the sleeping babe.

She had a tuft of golden blond hair, and according to her Papa, she had the hallmark blue eyes of the Fitzwilliams, but those could change as she got a little older. According to Lady Anne, little Tiffany was approximately the same size as Georgiana was when she was born.

"My best wishes on your betrothal, little brother," Andrew said as Richard admired his new niece. "Buck up, Richard, it is barely a fortnight until you see her again," Andrew ribbed his brother, who gave him a look that said, 'just you wait.'

"Has my nephew met my new niece yet?" Elizabeth asked as she admired the newest member of the family.

"Reggie is not two yet, so he does not know what to make of the little bundle he met earlier today," Andrew relayed. "I give him another year or so before he becomes a protective older brother."

"I will commiserate with Tiffany then," Elizabeth smiled, "I know all about having protective older brothers, who," she added, "are the best big brothers a girl could ever ask for."

"Were Jane and Perry not supposed to stop on their way?" Andrew asked.

"At the last overnight, Jane felt uncomfortable as she is so large and asked Perry if they could go right home. Poor girl, her feet are so swollen that she had had to beg off standing up with Lizzy," his mother informed Andrew.

"So who will have the honour of standing up with you, Sprite?" Andrew asked.

"Gigi," Elizabeth announced.

"William, I heard that you have taken orders and graduated near the top of your year at Cambridge; congratulations, brother," Andrew offered to the newly minted clergyman.

"It almost slipped my mind, Andrew," Elizabeth asked her brother, "when you meet with Mr. Beckman next, will you please ask if William would be allowed to perform our marriage ceremony?"

"There should be no objection, but I will not foist the decision on him," Andrew nodded once. "He knows Mr. Perkins at Pemberley intimately, and if he has agreed to take William on as a curate, that should be good enough for him."

"Thank you for your kind wishes, Andrew, and for agreeing to ask your rector if I may perform the marriage rites," William said as he took his time to admire the new Fitzwilliam.

Not long after, those who would be staying at Pemberley departed for the just over one-hour carriage ride to the Darcy estate. It was hard to part with Will, but Elizabeth consoled herself that she would see him on the morrow when Richard would take her to Pemberley. From there, a group of them would travel to Rivington and return the following day so that the new master and very soon-to-be mistress could look over the estate and meet the senior staff, servants, and some of the tenants. From her memory of the last time that she had been there, Lady Anne did not think that there was much lacking regarding décor, but as she told Elizabeth, their tastes may be very different.

~~~~~~~/~~~~~~~

The following day before they departed for Pemberley, Elizabeth and Richard visited with Marie after she had fed Tiffany. "Soon, you will be an old married woman just like me, Lizzy," Marie teased her sister-in-law.

"I am looking forward to that day with impatience, Marie. I am glad that you look so well less than three days after you gave us our Tiffany," Elizabeth answered. "She is so pretty."

"As her mother, I am bound to agree, but it will be hard to tell for many months how she will look," Marie pointed out. "And you, Richard, finally proposing to Retta. I believe that you two will do very well together. Andrew tells me you will go to Brookfield from Rivington?"

"That is my plan. I want to make sure that all is in order before

Loretta sees her future home. Lizzy will be well looked after with Uncle George, the rest of the family, and Mrs. Annesley," Richard replied.

"Did Aunt Anne agree to take on Mrs. Annesley to be Georgie's companion after your wedding, Lizzy?" Marie asked.

"She did. Gigi already knows and likes Mrs. Annesley very well," Elizabeth stated.

Not long after, Richard and Elizabeth were on their horses on the way to Pemberley with their expected escorts.

CHAPTER 12

Richard, Elizabeth, and Will rode their horses from Pemberley while the Darcy parents and Thomas and Tammy Bennet rode in one of the two carriages, with Aggie ensconced in the second carriage accompanied by the servants. Elizabeth's mother had remained at Snowhaven to be with Marie. The trip to Rivington was just a little over two hours. The estate was in a valley at the base of the Cloud Peak, close to the intersection of the borders of Derbyshire, Staffordshire, and Cheshire. Even though it was so close to the Peak District, there was a fair amount of flat land which the estate claimed.

The River Wheelock ran through the valley and was a tributary of the River Dane, itself a tributary of the River Weaver. The river was fed by water draining from the peaks, so there was never a water shortage at Rivington. From the gates, there was a two-mile ride to the floor of the valley, across a stone bridge over the River Wheelock, and then the drive rose until it reached a plateau where the manor house was situated.

The house, built in the Tudor style, was three stories tall and seemed to be about the same size as Longbourn. The senior staff was waiting to meet the estate's new owners as the carriages and horses were brought to a stop. Will introduced Elizabeth to the steward, Mr. Hector Belle, the housekeeper, Mrs. Beatrice Ralston, and the butler, Mr. Hubert Ellison. All three were long-serving staff at the estate and for the Darcys.

The rest of the servants were lined up in the entrance hall, where each one received a few words from the new mistress-to-be. Mrs. Ralston showed those at the estate for the first time to their suites. The Bennets, Richard, and Elizabeth were on the guest floor while the Darcys were on the family floor. After washing and changing, everyone except Aggie met back in the entrance hall, where the housekeeper commenced the tour. The dog decided on some much-needed sleep, so she stayed lying on the soft rug in her mistress' chambers.

The house was very well maintained. The Darcys used to be in residence for a few weeks a year, but the master and his son still visited a minimum of once a quarter to ensure their tenants' needs were addressed and to handle anything that might have come up. After they toured the public rooms on the ground floor, including the formal and family dining parlours, Elizabeth turned to Mother Anne. "I do not see anything that I desire to change. Like the décor at Pemberley, I find what you have done here much to my tastes."

"I could not agree with Lizzy more, Anne," Tammy added. "Just like Pemberley, everything is comfortable and inviting; I would call it understated elegance."

"It pleases me that you both feel that way; I think that you and Will shall do well here, Lizzy," Anne responded.

The mistress' and master's studies were on the first floor. A small storage area separated them, but the master's study was a huge space. "What say you, Lizzy, if we move your desk into this room, so we share the space and are not parted when we work at our desks? The study has enough size that we would be able to place your desk next to mine, and we would still have room between the desks and the walls to reach our seats comfortably," Will suggested.

"That is a good idea; I will enjoy working alongside you, Will," Elizabeth responded.

"That is more than enough, you two," Richard teased.

"Just you wait, Itch, soon Retta will be here, and then let us see who walks around like a besotted puppy," Elizabeth scoffed with a smile.

Also on the first floor was a rather well-stocked library, which, as Bennet pointed out, was no comparison to Pemberley's, but still more than enough to tempt him. The family sitting room and the school rooms were also on the first floor, the latter rooms connected with a door to the east side of the library.

The second floor was the family floor that had ten suites, in addition to the master suite. The nursery was next to the mistress' chambers with a connecting door on one side. On the other was a private sitting room, and beyond that was the master's suite.

The mistress' chambers were the only rooms that Elizabeth asked to be redecorated. The furniture was to her liking, but the colour scheme in pastels with a fair number of pink flowers was not. Elizabeth chose greens, some blue, and a touch of light yellow for the wall coverings and drapes.

When they walked through the master's chambers, Elizabeth looked with expectation at the huge bed within and hoped that Will would not want to spend their nights in separate chambers. Will had not put his stamp on his chambers yet, having just become master of the estate, but he was happy with the colours of hunter-green and browns used last time the room was redecorated.

Last, they walked about the third floor where the Bennets' and Elizabeth's chambers were. There was a total of twelve guest suites and a sitting room on the floor. Mrs. Ralston explained that the male servants had rooms in the attics while the female servants' rooms were near the kitchens.

The cook proved her worth to the new master and his fiancée that night when they all enjoyed a very well-cooked meal. Elizabeth, Lady Anne, and Tammy took turns entertaining in the music room after dinner, where there had been no separation of the sexes. Before everyone retired, Elizabeth expressed her approbation of Rivington and her belief that they would be content and happy starting their lives together there.

After a restful night's sleep, where both Elizabeth and Will had fallen asleep wishing they were already married and in each other's arms. They wished Richard a safe ride to Brookfield; the party began the return journey, though not all returned to Pemberley. The Bennet parents and Elizabeth had been invited to Longfield Meadows to look in on Jane, Perry, and Lady Rose. It seemed like the ideal opportunity, as the Rhys-Davies estate was less than three hours away.

~~~~~~~/~~~~~~~

Jane welcomed her parents and sister warmly as she reclined in her sitting room. Elizabeth was happy to see her sister looking so well, even if she could not stay on her feet too long at a time.

"There my babe goes again," Jane stated as she placed her hands on her belly, "This little one never rests and is already practicing dancing on my insides."

"That is how Marie was before she joined us," Lady Rose remembered, "Mayhap, you have another active young lady in your belly Jane."

"How did you like Rivington, Lizzy?" Jane asked, changing the subject.

"I liked it very well indeed. It is situated at the base of Cloud Peak and could not have a prettier prospect of the Peaks. It does not have as much forested area as Snowhaven for me to explore on my rambles and rides, but there is more than enough space for both, and Will and I are looking forward to long rides up to the crest of Cloud Peak," Elizabeth informed her sister.

"I cannot but agree with Lizzy, Jane." Tammy added, "It is a good situation, and there is almost naught that Lizzy needs to change in the house."

"Jane, has any progress been made on finding a location for the clinic, school, and home for children in Bedford yet?" Elizabeth asked.

"Yes indeed," Jane responded. "Mother Rose has been leading the effort given my girth and how hard it is for me to walk too far at any one time, so I will leave it to her to inform you of the progress that has been made."

"Working with Bedford's vicar and physician, we found structures to be used for all three. The buildings for the school and clinic are being refurbished as we speak, and we just purchased a house that will be able to house up to twenty children to start," Lady Rose reported.

"That is wonderful!" Elizabeth exclaimed. "We have found

facilities in Hilldale-on-Derwent, Matlock, Lambton, and Kympton. The project is exciting a lot of interest. Not only will it help the local populace, servants, and tenants of the surrounding estates, but it will offer several well-paying jobs that in turn will help support the town's economies."

"Are you still looking for land to build a house like the one Mama and the Meryton committee built where the Back children reside?" Jane asked.

"We will start the project after Will and I return from our wedding trip," Elizabeth informed her sister. "I have spoken to my mother, Mother Tammy, and Mother Anne, and I am going to request about fifty acres. I plan to create a mini-estate so that the children can help in any area that interests them, and then they can study in that direction as well. It will allow the children, who are already traumatised by losing their parents, to live the best lives that they can. In addition, we should try and place as many children with loving families who would like to adopt and make sure that siblings are not separated. The other ladies feel it is a sound plan. What are your thoughts, Aunt Rose and Jane?"

"Your plan has my full support," Jane stated.

"As you have mine too, Lizzy," Lady Rose stated. "Are you still considering moving the Black children to Derbyshire once the new facility is built?"

"As much as I would like to, I realise that it was my own selfish desire to have them near me that drove me to want them to be uprooted again. Unless I am told that they are not completely content with their new situation, or if they talk of wanting to move without my prompting, I will not ask to have them moved," Elizabeth explained.

"That is a very wise way of approaching the situation, Lizzy," Tammy agreed with the logic, as what is best is not always what one wants, and it took someone special to accept that.

"Jane, are you sure you will be well to attend my wedding?" Elizabeth asked, concerned for her older sister.

"I have foregone the betrothal ball as it is. If I rest well and keep off my feet, it will not be a hardship. I already had to cede my duties to stand up for you to Georgiana, but unless I enter my final confinement beforehand, I *will* be at your wedding, Lizzy," Jane said with determination. "It was very good of you and Will to ask William to officiate at your wedding; I know that he is much honoured by the request."

"The twentieth of June cannot arrive soon enough. Speaking of which, I am missing my betrothed so very much," Elizabeth shared.

Just after she spoke, Perry and Bennet entered the drawing room after the former had been showing the latter some new first editions acquired for the estate's library. And while it too did not rival Pemberley's, it was larger than Snowhaven's and a bookman's haven.

"Tammy and Lizzy, are you ready to depart? Do not forget we are expected at Pemberley for dinner tonight," Bennet pointed out. Within an hour, the carriage and security were on the road back to Pemberley.

~~~~~~~/~~~~~~~

Richard returned to Snowhaven a few days later, having made sure, more than once, that everything was to receive his betrothed and her family in about a sennight. He knew that being separated from Loretta would be trying, but he never expected it would be so hard as this. He thought of her anytime he was not busy with an occupation and missed her more than he could have imagined that he would miss someone outside of his immediate family.

He knew in a roundabout way that what he considered at the time was his sister's officious pleading with him to leave the military had led him to the happiness he had now. Until he resigned his commission, he had not allowed himself to be open to a future with a lady. He could not imagine making someone a war widow if it came to that. He thought about the conversation he had with Lizzy the day of his return to his brother's estate.

"Lizzy, may I speak with you?" Richard asked as he entered his sister's sitting room where her legs were curled under her as she read a book with Aggie snoring at her feet.

"*You know I always have time for you, brother,*" *she replied as she marked her place and put the book on a side table.*

"*Do you remember when you beseeched me to resign from the army Lizzy?*" *he asked.*

"*How could I forget!*" *she cried.* "*I must apologise profusely, Richard; it was not my place…*" *Richard leaned forward and placed his finger on his sister's lips to stop the verbal avalanche that he could see she was about to launch.*

"*First, let me say that you overstepped, Lizzy. If mother wanted to say something about my service, it was her place, not yours. You could have talked to me about your feelings and worries alone. Although my first reaction was to resent you and reject your words for talking to me about duty to family, given how duty has always been a driving force in my life, once I took the time to truly think about your words, I came to the conclusion that I was staying in the army for the wrong reasons.*" *Elizabeth had looked at him questioningly.* "*When I decided to choose the army, it was for the right reasons; I felt a calling as I told Mother and Father at the time.*

"*After Father was murdered, there was a little voice telling me that it was time to take up my estate, but I stubbornly refused to acknowledge what I knew was the correct path for me. You are not the only stubborn one on the family, Sprite,*" *Richard grinned.* "*After you spoke to me, I could no longer pretend not to hear the voice.*"

"*You do not resent me for begging you to leave the Dragoons, Itch?*" *Elizabeth asked tremulously,* "*I sincerely apologise for overstepping and talking for others when it was not my place to do so. I allowed my worry to overrule my good sense.*"

"*Your apology is accepted without reservation, little sister, and no, I do not resent you at all. On my honour, unless it was a path that I decided that I wanted to take, wild horses would not have dragged me and forced me to do that which I refused to do. You actually did me a favour by making me listen to what I knew was right for me,*" *Richard told a relieved Elizabeth.*

"*Retta?*" *Elizabeth asked.*

"*Yes, Loretta. If I were still in the army, I would not have considered her or anyone else as my life's partner, so in the end, it is the reason that I, in fact, want to thank you for waking me up out of the malaise that I had allowed myself to enter." Richard hugged and kissed his sister on her cheek before scratching Aggie behind the ears and then departing his sister's sitting room.*

~~~~~~~/~~~~~~~

The Bingleys and the Hursts arrived at Pemberley a day before the De Melvilles were expected. Martha Bingley had not accompanied her son, daughter, and their families as her mother was too frail for long-distance travel, and she did not want to leave her side for a few weeks, so she sent her apologies to her son.

Little Harry Hurst was almost two and a bundle of energy who seemed to like to run wherever he went and did so as soon as his nursemaid lowered him to the ground from the carriage. He was brought up short when he ran into Aggie, who looked at him with something akin to amusement as he fell onto his rear end after bouncing off the huge dog.

Will and Lizzy were just returning from a walk when they saw the little boy's collision with Aggie but smiled widely as Harry sat on the ground and stared in wonder at the huge dog that was sniffing him, so fascinated that he even forgot to cry at his unceremonious fall.

"Darcy, Lady Elizabeth, you both look well," Bingley intoned in his affable way as he saw the couple approaching the courtyard.

"Bingley, Mrs. Bingley, Hurst, and Mrs. Hurst, on behalf of my family, allow me to be the first to welcome all of you to Pemberley," Will returned. "I trust your journey was not too hard?"

"It was a good trip, thank you Mr. Darcy," Louisa replied as she watched her son's face being washed by Aggie as she licked him. Even more amusing was how tentative the nursemaid was, for she wanted to retrieve her charge but was not about to get too close to the enormous dog.

"Aggie heel!" Elizabeth commanded. After one last lick of the giggling boy who seemed to be quite enamoured with Aggie, she trotted to her mistress and plopped herself down next to Elizabeth's feet.

"Charles shared your letter, Mr. Darcy, about how Aggie was the hero when that disgusting man tried to importune Lady Elizabeth," Mandy Bingley stated.

"Please call me Lizzy; there is no need to stand on ceremony," Elizabeth requested.

"Thank you, Lizzy, please call me Mandy," She replied. "I have long loved your sister Jane as she often came to spend time with us."

"I am truly gratefully to have my sister and am glad you who needed her most was able to have her close by." Elizabeth again marvelled at her sister's ability to soothe those whose hearts were hurting.

"As you can see, Aggie is a gentle giant until someone threatens my betrothed. Should we continue this discussion inside?" Darcy suggested.

After the arriving guests greeted their host and hostess, they were shown up to their chambers on one of the guest floors by Mrs. Reynolds while the nursemaid with little Harry was directed to the guest nursery by a maid. Harry was not happy that his new 'fweind,' as he called Aggie, was not to accompany him but brightened when Elizabeth promised he would get to play with Aggie to his heart's content later.

The Bingleys and Hursts returned to the drawing room after washing off the dust from the road and changing out of their travel attire. While they were up in their chambers, the Bennets arrived with Lady Elaine accompanying them. The ladies sat together as the men made for the billiard room, except Bennet, who headed straight to the library.

"How is my friend Martha?" Tammy asked Louisa.

"She is well, Mrs. Bennet. She would have liked to be here to see Lizzy marry, but she will not leave Grandmama's side," Louisa explained.

"How does your grandmother Beckett do?" Tammy asked.

"She is as well as can be expected, but there was no question of her making such a journey as this one. She no longer travels, so Mama's siblings all come to visit at Netherfield now. It has been many months since the last time that Grandmama made the trip to her beloved Yorkshire," Louisa explained.

"I understand from Tammy that both you and Mrs. Bingley have joined the Meryton Committee and have been active in the endeavours around the Hertfordshire area," Lady Anne stated.

"We have," Mandy confirmed. "My sister and I have found the work very fulfilling, have we, not Louisa?" Louisa nodded vigorously. "It is sad how much need there is for the services that we offer. Mama told me about the update that was received from the Derbyshire Committee; it seems that you have made much progress."

"We have, and you are correct; there is much need, and we will do what we can do, but until it becomes a national priority, it will always be a drop in the bucket," Lady Elaine told the ladies.

"How are the Black children faring?" Elizabeth asked the question she had wanted to from the time the discussion began.

"They have adapted fully to their new surroundings and are flourishing," Mandy replied, "In fact, there is an adoption for them on the horizon."

"All seven of them?" Elizabeth asked in disbelief. Her first inclination was to think how they would never live near her, but that was but a moment as she knew adoption by a loving family would be the ideal for the children.

"Yes, all seven," Louisa confirmed.

"When did this come to pass?" Tammy asked, "I had no notion of this development until you mentioned it just now."

"Do you know Mr. and Mrs. Goodridge from Middlesex?" Louisa asked.

"Yes, they have a nice sized estate, Ashford Dale is the name, I believe, and no children," Tammy recalled.

"The very same," Mandy confirmed. "Evidently, they had wanted to adopt for a while now. They have no living family on either side and have never been able to have their own children. They visited the home where the Blacks are situated a little over a month ago, and evidently, they fell in love with them. Since the first visit, they have been back once or twice a week. They took the two oldest boys with them to see the estate the week before we left, and the two praised the situation to the sky when they returned.

"The Goodridges were preparing their home to receive the seven when we departed. I expect it will be just days until the children move to Ashford Dale permanently. They will be recognised as sons and daughters by the couple and take the Goodridge name. The oldest boy will be made the heir."

By the end of the recitation, Elizabeth had tears of joy streaming down her cheeks. "I could not have imagined a better outcome for them."

The discussion then moved to the upcoming wedding. As the conversation swirled about her, Elizabeth felt something akin to euphoria. One different decision and the boys would have ended up in gaol, and the other five would have been left to starve. She would see them occasionally, she was sure, but she knew that she would never have to worry for their futures again.

~~~~~~~/~~~~~~~

"Where is Fitzwilliam, Darcy?" Bingley asked after he took his shot.

"He returned to Brookfield today, and his betrothed and her family arrive there on the morrow. I never imagined that I would ever see him so besotted," Will replied as he lined up his shot.

"If that is not the pot calling the kettle black, then I do not know what would be," George Darcy ribbed his son.

"Are you saying that my friend walks around mooncalf, Mr. Darcy?" Bingley asked with a grin.

"That would be an understatement, Bingley," George responded, grinning at his son's discomfort. "You raised the subject of one being besotted with his betrothed, son. If I was inaccurate, you are welcome to correct me."

Will gave the three grinning men his best scowl. "May we just return to the game, please?"

"Peace, son. Have you informed Lizzy where you will go for your wedding trip yet?" George asked his son.

"No, I have not, Father; it is a surprise for her," Will replied.

"What are you planning, Darcy?" Hurst asked.

"I will share the information as long as you swear that you will not allow my wife to wheedle it out of you." Both Bingley and Hurst swore on their honour. "Perry has agreed to allow us to use his private vessel, which is berthed in Southampton. We will travel there from the wedding, and we will sail to the Italian peninsula. Lizzy was always fascinated by my descriptions of the area from when I was on my grand tour. If it were not for the war, I would have taken her to the Kingdoms of Portugal and Spain.

"I know she would also love to see France, but as the Great Terror has not ended, albeit it is less now than it was, I will not take a chance with my new wife by setting foot on any French lands."

"Given Lady Elizabeth's insatiable thirst for knowledge, I am sure that she will approve most heartily of the wedding trip," Bingley opined.

"All I need to do is make it until our departure without her drawing the information out of me," Will winced.

"You will hold strong while she uses her charms on you to loosen your lips, Will," his father stated.

"I truly hope so," Will replied. He wished his lips were otherwise engaged, for the word conjured many instances of their stolen kisses. He could not get enough of her lips, and when they kissed, he was at his most vulnerable but had managed to stop himself from revealing his plans—so far!

~~~~~~~/~~~~~~~

Richard had never been so nervous before. He had never ridden into battle, but he believed that he would have been calmer than he was as he waited for his love to arrive at his estate. He had gone over everything with his senior staff multiple times, and each time they had indulgently answered his questions as they assured him all was in place for the visit and that Brookfield would be displayed most advantageously.

He knew all was as it should be, but that did not quiet the inner voice of doubt that told him that Loretta would disapprove of his home. There was naught he could do now, for the De Melvilles would arrive on the morrow, so he could only pray that all would be well.

CHAPTER 13

Trying to contain his nervous energy, Richard stood under the portico, waiting for the carriages which sported the Jersey crest to come to a halt. He knew he had driven his staff to the edge of their patience and vowed he would reward them after, regardless of the outcome of this visit.

Richard was normally perfectly cool and calm in high-stress situations, but he had never stood on the precipice of matrimony before, nor had he ever welcomed someone of this import to his home, or anyone for that matter. To say that he wanted the visit to go well was an understatement.

The house, of similar size and style to the one at Rivington, was situated on rising ground. Richard's ancestors who founded the estate and built the house had cut out part of the hill to make the flat section of ground for the house; about a hundred yards from the rear of the edifice where the hill had been cut into it resembled a giant series of steps. There was an intricate drainage system utilising retaining walls and sluices in place that assured that water flowing down the rise would be diverted around the area where the manor house was built.

The time for worry was over as Richard stepped forward to welcome his betrothed and his in-laws-to-be as they exited the carriage. "Welcome, my L…Father Cyril and Mother Sarah, Loretta, and Wes," Richard bowed.

"I do not remember permitting you to address me so familiarly," Wes ribbed him, grinning. "I am sorry that I was away from home when you proposed to my baby sister; I missed my chance to work on you before my father consented."

"You may attempt if you like, *Wes*," Richard challenged, "but given our history, I am sure you remember how many times you tried and how you seldom succeeded in discomposing me."

"I could not think of a better man to marry my sister," Wes clapped Richard on the back.

"If you two hens are done clucking, mayhap you will lead me into my future house, Richard," Loretta said with a smile.

"Already henpecked, I see," Wes said near Richard's ear *sotto voce*. Wes backed away from Richard and knew that he would have to be careful; his soon-to-be brother-in-law would repay the courtesy when he least expected it.

Richard introduced the three senior staff to their soon-to-be mistress and her family. The housekeeper led the De Melville's to their chambers on the guest floor, the second floor. Once they had washed and changed, a footman led them back to the main entrance where Richard was waiting for them.

Besides the mistress' chambers, Loretta found little that was in urgent need of updating. Some of the décors were very much out of date, but she only asked for work to be done in the one or two rooms where the wall coverings were peeling. The same paper would be used, so the repaired rooms would match the rest. At some point in the future, if the master and mistress decided they wanted to do a major redecoration, colour and furniture changes would be considered.

As Loretta loved horses as much as he betrothed did, the highlight for her was when the steward showed them around the stables and explained the breeding programme that was one of Brookfield's biggest income producers.

Given the proximity to the peaks, there were not a lot of arable lands. Besides the home farm, only about fifteen percent of the land was allocated for agriculture, which was enough to grow vegetables, oats, and the grasses needed for hay. Not far from the stables were two large barns, and next to each one an equally large shearing shed, as long-haired merino sheep were herded in numbers at the estate. Lastly, cattle, both milk cows and those raised for food were kept on the estate.

As they sat in the drawing room after dinner, Loretta said, "Richard, I will be thrilled living here with you."

SHANA GRANDERSON A LADY

"I am most pleased to hear you say that, Loretta. The house-keeper and the butler will tell you that I was running around like a chicken with its head cut off as I was so worried that all should be in order for your visit," Richard owned.

"There was no need, Richard. So long as you are with me, any-where that we live will be home," Loretta assured him.

"As you are aware, we do not have a house in Town, but Andrew has gifted us Hilldale House to use at no cost as a wed-ding present, at least until Reggie comes of age," he informed his betrothed.

"It would be pleasant to have our own home in Town, but not so important as we have so many family members with town-houses. We could stay with one a season for close to ten years and not stay at the same one twice," Loretta joked.

The following day, Loretta, Richard, and Wes mounted their horses for the relatively short ride to Pemberley, where the De Melvilles would be hosted.

~~~~~~~/~~~~~~~

Georgiana was delighted; she was to be allowed to attend the ball in honour of Lizzy and Will. She would only be allowed to remain for one set after dinner and could only dance with fam-ily or close friends that her father approved beforehand.

Kitty Bennet was on the opposite end of the happiness spec-trum. As she was only fourteen, her mother and father had de-cided that she and Tom would not attend. Her parents explained that it would be her turn soon enough.

At fifteen, James had the same restrictions as Georgiana. He was pleased that he could attend, but it was not as big an event for him as it was for his cousin. He would stand up with his cousin Franny for the first, and he and Georgiana would dance the supper set. He could dance well, but like several boys his age, he had not had a major growth spurt yet, and his partner for the supper set would be a little taller than himself.

Graham Phillips was one and twenty. After Cambridge, where he read law, he had joined the firm of Norman and James at the Inns of Court where he was studying to become a barrister. He would have liked to have danced the first with Cara Long, who had just turned sixteen, but her father had claimed that honour, so, as she would have a shortened evening like the other young ladies and men not yet out in society, he had managed to secure the supper set with her.

The bulk of the guests started arriving two days before the ball. Most were being hosted at Pemberley as the family and friends that had been staying at the Darcy estate were now residing at Snowhaven.

There was a knock on the chamber door where Elizabeth was getting ready, and she nodded to her lady's maid to open it. "Marie! I am so glad that you came. Where are my niece and nephew?" Elizabeth asked.

"In the nursery while grandmothers and other relations visit, making the poor nursemaids superfluous. Tiffany is almost a month old, and it is such a short distance to Pemberley, making it an easy decision to be here," Marie informed her sister-in-law.

"Where is my brother Andrew?" Elizbeth asked.

"He is waiting in the attached sitting room to see his sister, who will be married in four days," Marie replied.

"Do you know what Will has planned for the wedding trip, Marie?" Elizabeth probed.

"Even if I did know, and I am not saying that I do, I would not tell you and spoil Will's surprise," Marie told Elizabeth, who put on a fake pout. "Lizzy, that deep burgundy silk gown is perfect for you. The short sleeves will help keep you cool on this warm summer's night."

"I am most pleased with all that Madam Chambourg produced for me. I thought that I owned many gowns before, but that was nothing to what was made for my trousseau. If I never need to be poked and prodded again, it will be far too soon!" Elizabeth was one of the rare breeds of lady that did not enjoy too much shopping. "I understand that Jane and Perry have remained at Snowhaven as my sister is fatigued. Was she well when you departed, Marie?" Elizabeth asked with concern.

"She seemed as well as could be expected, Lizzy. I agree with her decision about tonight; she wants to rest as much as she is able so that she will be able to attend your wedding," Marie responded.

"I cannot but agree with you, Sister. I would be a little sad if Jane were not with me when I marry Will," Elizabeth sighed dreamily as she was wont to do whenever she discussed marrying Will.

When Thénardier was happy that her mistress was just as she should be, Elizabeth stood, and she and Marie entered the sitting room. "You are definitely not a sprite any longer," Andrew said as he saw his sister.

"It only took you five years to determine that I had outgrown that nickname, brother?" Elizabeth arched her eyebrow as she smiled at Andrew.

"When will I outgrow 'Itch' *Sprite*?" Elizabeth heard from behind her. She turned to see Richard and Anne Ashby enter the sitting room.

"I will leave the four Fitzwilliam siblings," Marie said as she gave Elizbeth a light peck on the cheek, making sure not to undo any of the lady's maid's work.

"Did you manage to tear yourself away from Loretta's company?" Elizabeth teased Richard. "Anne, it so good to see you; you seem to have put on some weight," Elizabeth teased. It was the first time seeing her sister since she had announced that she was finally with child a month before.

"I love you too, Lizzy," Richard stopped himself from enfolding her in his arms as he did not want to run afoul of Thénardier as she watched closely from the bedchamber door.

"At your *ancient* age, I suppose that you are not Itch any longer, I will call you Richard or Rich. To me, you will always be my big brother Itch," Elizabeth conceded.

"If you two are done debating names, perhaps I could command your attention, little sister," Andrew asked dryly.

"Not before I ask Anne how she is doing in her state," Elizabeth replied.

"I am well, Lizzy, I was sick in the mornings for about a

month, but thankfully that has ceased. Ian and Amy send their regards and are looking forward to seeing you. Amy is especially excited as this is her first ball where she will attend the whole as she comes out in November," Anne informed Elizabeth.

"Now that I have greeted Anne and satisfied my curiosity, the floor is yours, brother," Elizabeth stated playfully.

"I thank you for your condescension, Lady Elizabeth," he replied sarcastically as Andrew gave her a put-on bow. "These are for you to wear tonight, Lizzy." Andrew removed a diamond and ruby necklace from a velvet case. It was a piece that she had never seen before. "These were part of Grandmama Fitzwilliam's jewels that were divided between Mother and Aunt Anne. Those that would have gone to her other daughter were held in trust and have been given to Anne. This one was part of the set that was given to Aunt Anne, and, based on your dress tonight, she has consented for you to wear the set."

"They are perfect," Elizabeth opined. "Thénardier, please assist me." There was a brooch in the form of a flower with diamonds for petals and a ruby at the centre. The tiara had many smaller diamonds with a large ruby at the apex. The necklace also had diamonds of increasing size until the two sides were joined by the biggest ruby that Elizabeth had seen, even larger than the one that she had worn at her coming out. The earbobs had four hanging diamonds with a ruby hanging a little below them.

Once her lady's maid was satisfied, Elizabeth walked into her dressing room and stood before the full-length mirror. She liked her ensemble very much, and there was just now one thing missing, in her opinion, Fitzwilliam Darcy standing next to her.

When she was escorted to her betrothed, who was waiting in the hall outside her chambers, he was struck all over again at just how stunning Elizabeth was.

It was a long receiving line comprised of Darcys, Fitzwilliams, and Bennets, with the betrothed couple the last in the line before the guests entered the glistening ballroom. After a little over an hour, the last of the guests had moved through the line, and the family, who had been standing and greeting one and all, moved into the ball room.

"I suppose my mother had the right of it, that it would not look right if I danced every set with you, Lizzy," Will sighed forlornly.

"We are dancing the three most important dances, after all, so you have naught to repine. I expect to see you dancing with others tonight, Will," Elizabeth returned.

"You know I do not like to dance with someone unless I am acquainted with them," Will responded with put-on pique.

"And I suppose," Elizabeth smiled as they used the words from an argument some years before, "that one is not able to be introduced at a ball. You know practically everyone here, so even if you were still that way, you would have no valid excuse tonight."

"You remember I told you about the dance, the Waltz, that I learnt on my grand tour, do you not?" Will asked quietly, and Elizabeth nodded. "It is a great pity that polite society refuses to countenance it here in England; how I would love to dance it with you tonight, my love." Will dreamed of Elizabeth in his arms as he guided her around the room in the rise and fall of the forbidden dance.

"You scandalise me, Will Darcy! I could never see myself dancing such an intimate dance in public," Elizabeth arched her eyebrow at Will while her eyes shone, imagining how good it would feel in his arms, in a dance, or any other reason for him holding her.

"I will teach it to you when we are alone after we marry. I swear that we will dance it on our wedding trip, Lizzy." He had not lied to her; they would dance the Waltz, but not alone, with other couples on their wedding trip to the Italian peninsular.

Richard and Loretta also would have preferred more than three sets but resigned themselves to Aunt Anne's rule that no more than three sets with one who was married or betrothed to the requester. A little more than a month after Lizzy and Will married, they would be man and wife when none could gainsay them again.

All too soon, the ball ended. The younger girls and boy all enjoyed their allowed time at the dance and left after the set after supper without complaint. Georgiana particularly had enjoyed her supper very well that night, sitting with James Bennet.

The day after the ball, Elizabeth and her mother met with Lady Anne and Georgiana, and it was decided that with Mrs. Annesley's approval, she would make the move from Snowhaven to Pemberley the day of the wedding. Elizabeth would be sad to see the lady depart, but she was happy that she would now be with Gigi.

~~~~~~~/~~~~~~~

Will had a 'stag party' of sorts the night before his wedding. All the younger men met in the billiards room while most of the ladies were at Snowhaven. Will missed not seeing his love that day, but he would never have to leave her side again in little more than twelve hours.

He and the rest of the men had the midday meal at Snowhaven after a rehearsal in the church in Matlock with William Bennet. If one did not know that it was his first time performing the marriage rites, they would not have been able to tell from the confident way the new clergyman conducted the practice service.

After Will took his leave from Elizabeth, he and some of the men returned to Pemberley. He could not wait for the wedding to be over so he would not have to part from her again.

"Will!" Andrew snapped him out of his reverie. "If it were anyone but you, I would be admonishing him about not hurting Lizzy, but I am sure that you would lay down your life so she would not experience any pain. Do you know that after his anger wore off when he thought that you had inappropriate thoughts about his little girl, my father predicted that you would be her choice of husband one day?"

"No, I was never informed of that, but it makes me feel even better to know that I would have had Uncle Reggie's blessing," Will replied.

"My father will be looking down on us tomorrow, and he will be as happy and proud as any father could be," Andrew said, missing his father especially now before he was to give Elizabeth away. "I look forward to being able to call you brother on the morrow, Will." Andrew clapped his cousin on the back.

"If you and Lizzy are half as happy as Mandy and me, you will have the most felicitous of marriages, Darcy," Bingley said as he sat down, a little in his cups. "Do you need any pointers, well you know—about the wedding night," Bingley grinned as he asked his friend the question.

"Thank you, Bingley, but I am not an innocent, so I *do not* need any advice in that area. I think it is time for us to head for our bedchambers, for it would not do for you to be in your cups at my wedding in the morning." As he had in the past, when he saw his friend in his cups, Will was amused at his antics in that state.

"Have no fear, brother-to-be," Richard said as he and Will headed to their chambers, "I will make sure that you are at the church well ahead of the required time. It is an honour to stand up with you, Will."

"The honour is mine, Richard; you have always been more of a brother than a cousin, and on the morrow, it will be official. And I get to return the favour when it is your turn at the altar. It is not like we will never see each other, with barely an hour by carriage between our estates there will be ample opportunity for visits after your wedding trip.

~~~~~~~/~~~~~~~

The night before her wedding, after the gathering of all of the ladies broke up, Elizabeth's mother and Mother Tammy came to her to talk to her about what to expect on the wedding night.

"Like your papa and me, you and Will have the deepest kind of love, Lizzy, and when there is love, then everything that you need in the relationship is built on a solid foundation. You respect each other, and he will never do anything to occasion your pain if he can help it," her mother stated.

"You have grown up on an estate, so you know that the male

appendage will be inserted inside of you, do you not?" Mother Tammy asked. Blushing all shades of red and pink, Elizabeth nodded. "I am sure with your voracious reading that you have read a book or two on the subject, am I correct?" Again, Elizabeth nodded.

"With the love that you two have, He will not want to merely take his pleasure and then leave you; in fact, I am almost sure that it will be his preference to sleep every night in the same bed as you. Have you two canvassed the subject?"

"Yes," came the mortified squeak. "We will share a bed."

"Then the most important thing will be communication," Mother Tammy added.

"What Tammy said is absolutely correct. Do not be afraid to tell him what you find pleasurable and what you do not. Also, ask him the same for himself," Lady Elaine explained.

"If I take pleasure in the act, will I not be wanton?" Elizabeth asked, not able to look either lady in the eye.

"No, Lizzy, never!" her mother cried. "When the act is within the bounds of marriage and love, there will never be anything wrong with both of you taking pleasure, regardless of where, as long as you have privacy, or when! Please do not buy into the nonsensical tale that a woman 'must lie still' while her husband does what he does. Mayhap in the worst kind of arranged marriages, but *not* in a love match like yours, like mine, or Aunt Anne & Uncle George, your Mother Tammy and Father Bennet, and I could go on and on.

"It is not written anywhere that the man is the only one who should have pleasure in the marital bed; you are as entitled to take pleasure as your husband, and that makes you happy, not wanton!"

"We will not lie to you Lizzy, the first time could occasion you some pain, and there will be some blood, but *only* the first time; each time, it will get easier. It is like anything else in life; if you want to be proficient, you must practice diligently," Mother Tammy teased her birth-stepdaughter.

"Do you have any questions, Lizzy?" her Mama asked.

"No, Mama, Mother Tammy. You were very thorough in your explanations, and I think I will try to get some sleep now." Elizabeth kissed both ladies on the cheek, and after her lady's maid assisted her in preparing for bed, she eventually allowed sleep to claim her as she dreamed about sharing a bed with Will and what they would do in said bed.

Elizabeth looked over at Aggie, who was where she would expect to find her, stretched out on the thick rug and no doubt dreaming of chasing rabbits. She would be nine soon but still seemed to be in good health. She was a little slower and did like to rest more than she used to, but other than that, all seemed well with the dog that Elizabeth loved to distraction. One of the signs that Elizabeth knew to be wary of was when Aggie would start to eat less and not be as interested in her food. Thankfully, Aggie would still wolf down her food and never looked the other way when offered a treat. Both Aggie and Saturn would move to Rivington just before the master and mistress of the estate were scheduled to return from Loretta and Richard's wedding.

CHAPTER 14

Will woke up before sunrise. It was two hours to the church at Matlock, but to be safe, he had demanded that the younger men who had stayed with him at Pemberley be ready to depart at a quarter before seven. The wedding was to commence and half past the hour of nine, and he cared not if he had to wait, but he would *not* be late for the wedding to the woman that he loved more than he could aptly describe.

Andrew had returned to Snowhaven with the aid of a full moon after the stag party, leaving Richard, Bingley, and Wes as Will's escorts. Perry would have been present if not for his care of his wife.

As if he had a bell around his neck, Carstens entered the bedchamber before Will's feet reached the ground. Will had no idea how his valet knew when he rose from his bed regardless of what time it was, but he always did. He assisted his master to bathe in steaming hot water and then shaved Will as close as could be. Next, he assisted in dressing the groom in a deep navy-blue suit with a shimmering white waistcoat. Last were the black shoes that Carstens had polished to perfection.

Will made his way down to the breakfast parlour as the first glimmer of the approaching dawn was visible out of the east-facing windows. He had expected that a footman would have to be dispatched to wake his three escorts, especially as at least two of them had been somewhat in their cups, so it was a complete surprise when he entered to three grinning men all sipping coffee.

"And here I thought that you would be the first of us ready this morning; mayhap the day is not as important to you as the rest of us," said Richard.

"You know how Darce has to primp and preen before the mirror," Bingley added his jibe.

"We were worried that you had changed your mind," Wes added with a grin.

"Just you wait, Richard, when you are nervous on the day of your wedding, I will pay you back tenfold," Will retorted good-naturedly.

"I would expect nothing less, Will," Richard smirked.

"Is everything planned for your wedding trip?" Wes asked.

"It is. I have a full floor at a very good inn just outside of Birmingham reserved for tonight; it will be a little more than forty miles of travel. The next day we will go about eighty miles to Oxford, leaving us less than sixty miles to Southampton the day after next as we will not travel on the Sabbath. We will board Perry's ship early in the morning on Tuesday the five and twentieth day of June and will sail with the tide that morning," Will informed the three.

"Lizzy will love the trip you have planned, Will. You know how much she had desired to travel and see some of the places that she had learnt about," Richard opined.

"Which is why I planned it as I did. Keeping the plans secret from Lizzy has not been easy." Will was about to add 'when she withholds her kisses,' but with Richard standing before him, he decided that discretion was the better part of valour.

As they were ready, the men entered the waiting carriage at just after half past the hour of six as the first tendrils of the sun's fingers were steaking across the eastern sky, heralding the rising sun.

~~~~~~~/~~~~~~~

Elizabeth had her most vivid dream of being with Will that she had ever had and woke up with a distinct longing for him. She was sure that the talk that she had with her Mama and Mother Tammy the night before had influenced her dream. She did not feel like a wanton, thanks to the words spoken by the two women and their assurances when they had their discussion. Rather than apprehension, like so many young brides, Elizabeth was looking forward to her wedding night with anticipation.

Andrew and Father Bennet would accompany her in the carriage to the Matlock church. It was less than two miles to the church, so it would be a quick ride. Elizabeth smiled as she remembered how her mother had checked and then rechecked with Mrs. Smythe that everything was planned and ready for the wedding breakfast, which was to be held in Snowhaven's ball room.

Elizabeth sat on the edge of her bed and rang for her lady's maid just as the sun was creeping over the horizon. It was well before seven, but there was a lot to do to get ready before she departed for the church. Having anticipated the time that her mistress would start to prepare, Thénardier arrived within a minute of her mistress pulling the bell pull and informed Lady Elizabeth that her bath would be ready in moments.

As Elizabeth sat in her robe after her bath, there was a knock on the door, and her mother, Marie, Mother Anne, and Mother Tammy entered her room. "Did you manage to sleep at all, Lizzy?" her mother asked.

"Not so very much, Mama," Elizabeth responded. "I am too excited for sleep."

"You have more than enough helpers, so I will return to my chambers to dress, but I could not start the day without seeing you, Sister," Marie stated as she kissed her sister-in-law on the cheek then departed the chambers.

"What a bride you will make today, Lizzy," Mother Anne gushed as Thénardier hung the dress on a hook in preparation for Elizabeth to don it.

The colour of the groom's waistcoat matched the dress. It was a simple sparkling white dress with an empire waist and puffed sleeves with a band of Belgium lace around the bottom edge. There was a gossamer overlay that had a few pearls worked into it that would match the pearl necklace and earbobs that she would be wearing—gifts from Mother Tammy and Father Bennet. Elizabeth had forgone a wedding bonnet for a gossamer veil with pearls and a very few diamond chips that would sparkle in the light. It was exactly the dress that Elizabeth wanted as she did not favour too many embellishments; the bit of lace on her sleeves was more than enough for her.

"I could not agree more. The contrast of the colour of your hair with the dress will be stunning," Mother Tammy opined.

"It is my wedding day, so you will do anything to help me?" Elizabeth asked the three women cryptically as she arched her eyebrow. "Where is Will taking me for my wedding trip?" Elizabeth's persistence made all three giggle like the girls they were many years ago.

"We will help with anything that you *need* to get ready before your wedding, Lizzy," her mother replied. "Knowing where Will is taking you is not one of them. Let him surprise you, and besides, you will know soon enough.

Elizabeth sighed when her latest attempt to gain the intelligence was rebuffed. She did not mind being surprised, but her curiosity would not allow her to give up until the moment that she decided to follow her mother's advice; it was her wedding day, after all.

~~~~~~~/~~~~~~~

Will and his three attendants arrived at the church just under an hour before the time that he had to be there. Knowing that Will at least would have been barred entrance to Snowhaven before the ceremony, and with the men not wanting to leave Will to wait on his own, all accompanied him to the church. The pews started filling up about half an hour before the ceremony.

Mr. Beckman and William Bennet entered the church from the rectory and showed Will and Richard to the room off the altar where they could wait and sit out of the arrival congregants' view.

"I know that you have known my sister her whole life," William said seriously to Will, "just remember that she has a cadre of brothers who will be willing to deal with you if you ever do anything to hurt Lizzy."

"If you knew Will as well as I do, you would know that it is not in his nature to hurt anyone intentionally, especially not one who he loves like our sister," Richard defended Will.

"That I believe," William stated, "but as one of her older brothers, I felt that I had to say something. Now it is done, we can move on with the most pleasant task that I have before me. I meant no offence, Will."

"No offence taken, William. I would not have expected less and would do the same with the man who one day has the honour of being accepted by Georgie," Will returned as he extended his hand to shake William's to back up his words with action.

William left the two cousins alone, and about twenty minutes later, he poked his head through the door to tell them it was time to take their places.

~~~~~~~/~~~~~~~

The carriages bearing the family from Snowhaven arrived, and their passengers had all filed out a little before the one bearing Elizabeth, Andrew, and Bennet arrived. After the last of the family, excepting Georgiana, entered and took their seats in the front pews, the doors to the vestibule were closed. The doors were opened again briefly, and Georgiana made her way up the aisle towards her position opposite Richard. William Bennet was struck at how beautiful Miss Darcy was as she glided towards her spot with measured, slow steps.

Once Miss Darcy was in place, William gave a nod to the string quartet leader, and they played a flourish. As they did, William gave the sign for the congregation to stand. The doors to the vestibule opened, and with Andrew on her right and Father Bennet on her left, Elizabeth started the walk toward her destiny, to the love of her life, to finally join with her Will.

Will knew that Elizabeth was beautiful, but he had never seen her looking more so than she did as she walked toward him. She gave him a saucy look that promised much love, laughter, and pleasure to come for the rest of their lives, and at last, he understood why Carstens had insisted on the waistcoat that he was wearing, as it matched her gown perfectly.

For her part, Elizabeth looked directly at Will's eyes and held his gaze as she was guided up the aisle. Will was more handsome than any man deserved to be, but to her, on this day, he looked like a god amongst men. She watched as he approached them as they had stopped near the altar. Father Bennet lifted her veil and kissed the cheek on his side, and Andrew had done the same on the other, then Andrew had placed her arm on Will's while Bennet took his seat in the pews with his wife and other children.

As they approached the altar, Elizabeth drew near to Jane, who took her hand and squeezed it for support. Elizabeth stopped for a second next to her older sister, sharing a knowing look only they could interpret, then Will led her to a position in front of William, who gave the sign for the congregation to be seated.

William opened the Book of Common Prayer and began the liturgy.

"Dearly beloved, we are gathered together here in the sight of God, and in the face of this congregation, to join together this Man and this Woman in holy Matrimony; which is an honourable estate, instituted of God in the time of man's innocence, signifying unto us the mystical union that is betwixt Christ and his Church; which holy estate Christ adorned and beautified with his presence, and first miracle that he wrought, in Cana of Galilee; and is commended of Saint Paul to be honourable among all men: and therefore is not by any to be enterprised, nor taken in hand, unadvisedly, lightly, or wantonly, to satisfy men's carnal lusts and appetites, like brute beasts that have no understanding; but reverently, discreetly, advisedly, soberly, and in the fear of God; duly considering the causes for which Matrimony was ordained.

"First, it was ordained for the procreation of children, to be brought up in the fear and nurture of the Lord, and to the praise of his holy Name.

"Secondly, it was ordained for a remedy against sin, and to avoid fornication; that such persons as have not the gift of continency might marry and keep themselves undefiled members of Christ's body.

"Thirdly, it was ordained for the mutual society, help, and

comfort, that the one ought to have of the other, both in prosperity and adversity. Into which holy estate these two persons present come now to be joined. Therefore, if any man can shew any just cause, why they may not lawfully be joined together, let him now speak, or else hereafter forever hold his peace.

"I require and charge you both…"

The service flew by in a blur, and before they knew it, they were reciting their vows as they took each other's hands:

"I, Fitzwilliam George Darcy, take thee, Elizabeth Rose Bennet Fitzwilliam to be my wedded Wife, to have and to hold from this day forward, for better for worse, for richer or for poorer, in sickness and in health, to love and to cherish, till death us do part, according to God's holy ordinance; and thereto I plight thee my troth."

"I Elizabeth Rose Bennet Fitzwilliam take thee, Fitzwilliam George Darcy to my wedded Husband, to have and to hold from this day forward, for better for worse, for richer or for poorer, in sickness and in health, to love, cherish, and to obey," Lizzy paused, gave Darcy a saucy look and continued, "till death us do part, according to God's holy ordinance; and thereto I give thee my troth."

The couple released each other's hands, as Richard placed the ring on William Bennet's open Bible pages. William blessed the ring before handing it to Will, who took the ring and placed it on the fourth finger on Lizzy's left hand, saying:

"With this Ring I thee wed, with my Body I thee worship, and with all my worldly Goods I thee endow: In the Name of the Father, and of the Son, and of the Holy Ghost. Amen."

After the giving and receiving of the ring, they knelt as William intoned a prayer of blessing. Once the prayer was complete, he joined their right hands together and said:

"Those whom God hath joined together let no man put asunder.

"Forasmuch as *Fitzwilliam* and *Elizabeth* have consented together in holy Wedlock and have witnessed the same before God and this company, and thereto have given and pledged their troth each to the other and have declared the same by giving and receiving of a Ring, and by joining of hands; I pronounce that they be man and wife together, In the Name of the Father, and of the Son, and of the Holy Ghost. Amen.

"God the Father, God the Son, God the Holy Ghost, bless, preserve, and keep you; the Lord mercifully with his favour look upon you; and fill you with all spiritual benediction and grace, that you may so live together in this life, that in the world to come ye may have life everlasting. *Amen*

It was done; they were married; all that was left was to sign the register. With Georgiana and Richard in tow, the newly married Darcys followed Mr. Beckman into the vestry and into the room on the other side of the door where the register was kept. Will signed first, and then Elizabeth signed her maiden name for the last time.

"Finally, you are my sister, Lizzy," Georgiana gushed as she congratulated her sister then her brother.

"Do not forget that you have gained a bunch of new brothers and sisters today, Gigi," Elizabeth said as she accepted the well wishes.

"Including this old ex-soldier," Richard grinned.

"Alex will be happy to have so many brothers now, especially as some of them are around his age," Will opined.

"Georgie and I will leave you now," Richard said as he took his new younger sister's arm.

"Why are Will and Lizzy not joining us?" Georgiana asked in her innocence. She received no answer as Richard closed the door behind him after propelling Georgiana back into the church.

The newlyweds shared a small laugh at their sister's expense, and then Will drew his wife into arms. "Mrs. Darcy," he said reverently.

"Mr. Darcy," Elizabeth returned softly.

Their lips met hungrily, and had they not been aware of the family members waiting for them on the other side of the door, they may have allowed themselves to go far beyond just one.

Will's one hand roamed over her back which elicited a little sigh from his wife while his other held her close to him, and in response, her arms found themselves around her husband's neck.

After about five minutes, they broke apart and put themselves to rights. Once they were ready, Will opened the door leading to the church and led his bride inside. Will was met by his parents and siblings, while Elizabeth fell into her mother's arms with her brothers, sister, and sister-in-law awaiting their turns. The Rhys-Davies and Bennets were just behind the Fitzwilliams.

After Alex wished his brother and new sister joy, he looked around at the family, waiting for their turns to wish the ecstatic couple joy as well. "All of the Bennets and Fitzwilliams are now my brothers and sisters?" He asked hopefully, and his mother nodded. "Does that make my uncles and aunts additional parents as well?" asked the twelve-year-old boy.

"No, my son," Lady Anne replied, "you still only have your father and me as parents; the rest will remain your uncles and aunts." She laughed when Alex still looked a little sceptical. "Find me at the wedding breakfast, Alex, and I will explain it to you."

"You are a Darcy now, Lizzy," Andrew drawled as he hugged his sister.

"I am, but I will also be a Fitzwilliam for all time, Andrew," Elizabeth promised as she returned his hug and kissed his cheek.

"You are next," Elizabeth whispered in Richard's ear as she hugged him.

The Bennets replaced Anne after she had hugged her younger sister. First, Elizabeth went to where her older sister was sitting; Jane's smile was radiant as she looked at her sister so full of excitement before her.

"God was very good to us when he guided us to meet one another. You are a bride of incomparable beauty, Lizzy," Jane told her as she hugged her sister as close as she could, given her girth, "I am so happy that this active babe waited so that I could attend your wedding. You will excuse me if Perry takes me directly home and not to the wedding breakfast, will you not?"

"Of course I understand, Janey; I hope that all will be well,"

Elizabeth replied, her concern evident as she searched her sister's features.

"The pains have just begun, there are many hours yet, but it is time to leave," Jane said as she winced a little.

After a brief discussion among the family, it was decided that Tammy would leave with her daughter, Perry, and Lady Rose. Everyone followed them out and wished them an easy trip and hoped that Jane would gain her home before the babe was ready to make its appearance. Perry had one of his grooms ride ahead to notify the midwife and doctor that their services were needed by the Duchess of Bedford forthwith.

After they departed, the remaining family members entered their carriages for the short ride to Snowhaven and the tables that were groaning under the weight of the delectable food awaiting one and all at the celebratory meal.

CHAPTER 15

The newlywed couple left the church a few minutes after the rest of the carriages to give the family time to get to the ballroom ahead of them. They were in an open chaise pulled by a matched set of white horses decorated with many white ribbons; the picture it made was completed by the sight of Biggs and Johns riding on the back. The two would eventually go with their mistress to her new estate, but first, they would be two of the footmen who accompanied the couple on their wedding trip. The only change for the two huge men would be the colour of the livery.

The road was lined in places with Snowhaven's tenants, who had come out to wave to Lady Elizabeth and Mr. Darcy on their ride back to the manor house. When they arrived under the portico, they were met by a footman and Mr. Smythe, who looked indulgently on the bride he had known her for the last seventeen years of her life.

Will and Elizabeth followed the butler to the ballroom's doors, and Mr. Smythe nodded to the two footmen who were posted to open the doors wide. He then marched a few feet into the room and struck the floor with his staff three times. "Mr. Fitzwilliam Darcy and his wife, Lady Elizabeth Darcy," Smythe announced with pride.

The glowing couple walked into the ballroom to rousing cheers as the butler exited and the doors were closed, and it was but seconds before well-wishers inundated them. As was their duty, the next hour was spent walking around the room accepting well wishes and saying a few words to each who offered them.

At some point, Loretta and Richard took pity on the newlyweds and led them to where the family and close friends were congregated. Loretta sat down with them and was soon joined by Georgiana, Kitty, and Amy. Richard returned with two plates and some glasses of lemonade.

"Eat and drink!" he commanded. As soon as he said it, both Elizabeth and Will realised that they had not eaten anything yet, only a little to drink in their excitement. They were grateful for the selection of pastries and little meat pies that Richard had chosen for them. Both ate hungrily.

"Slow down, Lizzy," Loretta advised, "or you will be wearing more cake than you are eating."

"I am going to miss you and Will so much," Georgiana owned. "It will not be until Retta and Richard's wedding that I will see you again."

"We will be there a few days before the wedding, Gigi, so it will not be *that* long," Elizabeth teased her newest sister, and Georgiana affected a fake pout.

Feeling refreshed after eating, the bride and groom struck out once more into the crowd to make sure that no one would leave feeling slighted or overlooked.

Toasts were offered first by Andrew and then by Bennet. After the toast and before Elizabeth went up to change, her birth father had a word with her. "Being at your wedding is one of many things that I did not dare to dream would ever happen for me. And walking you down the aisle, even sharing the duty with Andrew, was a pleasure that is hard to describe in mere words," Bennet told his daughter.

"Just because I am married does not mean that you will not see me, Father Bennet. Besides, we can still play chess by post, and I promise not to play as hard as I can," Elizabeth teased her birth father.

"What a wonderful young woman you are, Lizzy; you are a credit to your mother and late father." He offered quietly.

Mention of her beloved papa warmed Elizabeth's heart as she believed with all her being that although she could no longer see him, that he was always with her. "I am sure that Papa would have loved today," Elizabeth said.

Bennet kissed his second daughter on the forehead, and she went up to the chambers of her youth for the last time to change into her travelling attire as Bennet rounded up his children save one. When the newlyweds departed, they, the Gardiners, and the Phillipses would all hie to Longfield Meadows. William would make the ride on the morrow.

As the large and comfortable Darcy carriage stood ready, Elizabeth farewelled her family members until she arrived at her mother, the last in line to talk to her before she was to board the equipage. "I will miss you, Mama," Elizabeth owned.

"And I will miss you, Lizzy, but you are to have a wonderful honeymoon, and I promise that you will miss none of us as much as we will miss you. Just remember what I told you and let the love that you have for one another guide you," Elaine told her daughter and kissed both cheeks. "Now away with you two. Will, look after my baby," Elaine reminded him.

"You have my promise, Mother Elaine," Will replied. Then he followed Elizabeth into the carriage and tapped the roof, and with a little bit of a jerk, they were off. Elizabeth had opened the window and leaned out, waving until the family was out of sight.

"Alone at last," Will said as he reached around Lizzy to help her slide the window closed and replaced the curtain. The natural arching of her head to look at him was too much an invitation to ignore, so he kissed his wife.

"Will, you did not tell me where we are to go, or at least our destination today, Will?" Elizabeth asked when he pulled back and again looked down at her.

"Yes, my love, we are for the Golden Cock Inn outside of Birmingham, which is about forty miles distant," he disclosed. "I have the whole floor reserved, so we will not be disturbed by any other guests—nor will we disturb anyone," Will murmured, his look heated as he soaked her in, and she blushed in expectation of all that was to come, appreciating his thoughtfulness anew.

She rewarded him with a kiss, revelling in the fact that they did not have to hold themselves back from all they had longed to share. His hands roamed over his wife's body, and he swelled with pride when he heard her gasp of pleasure as his hands grazed her pert nipples through her thin day dress. She pressed into it in a bid for more, so after pulling the dress off her shoulders, he slid his finger under both the dress and chemise to cup her breast. He groaned at the feel of it, both firm and pliant, and that it filled his large hand, giving her what she asked for when his thumb pad slid over her nipple, and she arched her back in enjoyment, unconsciously offering him more.

Long aware of his need of her, she wanted to gift him the same, so her hand slid along his length, his trousers unable to save him from the feel of her exploration, which caused her husband to groan even as he kissed her deeper in response to the pleasure. "What you do to me, Lizzy," Will's ragged breath made her smile. "As impatient as I am to consummate our marriage, I do not want it to be in the coach for the first time. Mayhap we can talk about something that will not arouse our passions so that we can make the Golden Cock with our clothes on." Seeing the disappointment in his wife's eyes, he kissed her quickly and grinned. "After tonight, all bets are off, so long as we have privacy. I want only me to ever see you so impassioned."

His promise made her smile as she wanted no other woman to see him thusly. They disentangled themselves, leaned against the squabs holding hands, began to discuss their wedding.

~~~~~~~/~~~~~~~

The group that departed Snowhaven for Longfield Meadows arrived some three hours later. They were met by Perry, who stated that the doctor and the midwife were with Jane, as were their mothers. Maddie Gardiner and Hattie Phillips made their way up to the birthing suite, while the rest of the family kept Perry distracted as much as they were able.

"This is all Perry's fault," Jane yelled as a massive pain wracked her body. "He did this to me!"

"It will not be too much longer, your Grace," the midwife promised Jane, understanding that she just wanted that huge babe out of her body. The doctor waited in the attached sitting room just in case he was needed.

"All will be well, Janey. It will be like it has been for women throughout time who have come through the travails of childbirth and eventually able to tell the tale with a rueful smile," Tammy soothed her daughter.

"I have brought four children into the world, Jane, and I am mostly the same as I ever was," Aunt Maddie told her sweetest niece.

"When you were in the throes of labour, I am sure that is *not* what you wanted to hear, now was it?" Jane replied curtly as the next pain tore through her body.

"I see the 'ead, your Grace. On the next pain, I want you to push for all you are worth," the midwife ordered. When it started, Jane bore down with all of her might. "Again, your Grace, as 'ard as you can, the babe's shoulders are out!"

Jane complied and was rewarded with the lusty cries of her newborn babe. "What is it?" Jane asked as she lay back, thankful that the ordeal was over.

"*He* is a healthy boy, Jane," Lady Rose reported as she assisted the nursemaid to clean her grandson, the new Marques of Birchington.

"'E is not as big as I would 'ave expected, given 'ow big your belly was, your Grace," the midwife puzzled.

"Have you picked a name as yet?" Hattie Phillips asked.

"We have not, Aunt Hattie." Jane sighed in relief. A son or daughter had not mattered, just that she and Perry were able to share the joy of parenthood. "We wanted to wait and see what we were gifted with before…Ohhhhh! Why are the pains starting again?" Jane asked fearfully.

"That would be the after…" The midwife froze in midsentence, as on further examination, she saw a head crowning. "Push, your Grace, push with everything that you 'ave," she instructed. The second babe took far less effort than the first, then a higher-pitched cry was heard in the birthing chamber.

"A girl with a mop of blond hair already, while her poor

brother is bald," Tammy turned to show Jane her daughter and almost panicked, as Jane had lost consciousness. It took a moment before she could gather her thoughts then remembered that when she had laboured with Kitty and Tom, she too had lost consciousness for a while right after the birth, and Thomas had panicked the whole time.

The doctor examined the duchess after she had been cleaned up and dressed in a new night gown. "In my opinion, her Grace is simply sleeping as she is exhausted and should wake any time…" even as the doctor was giving his prognosis, Jane's eyes flicked open.

"Is my son well?" she asked as her mother and Mother Rose helped her into a sitting position.

"He is very well, Jane, and so is your daughter!" Aunt Maddie informed her niece, amused at the momentary shock.

"Daughter? Two?" the Duchess asked incredulously.

"Yes, you delivered two babes daughter—an heir and his sister," Lady Rose gushed as she handed her grandson to his mother. Jane offered him a breast, and he latched on hungrily. "I am happy that you and my son hired a wetnurse for the night feedings; you will need help now that there are two mouths to feed."

"Is my daughter well?" Jane asked, searching for her now that he was settled.

"Very much so," Tammy promised her daughter while looking at her granddaughter lovingly. "She is smaller than her brother, but she is as healthy as any of the babes that I bore. With Kitty and Tom, it was the other way around but now look at them. They are as healthy as any other children."

"Mother Rose, will you please ask my husband to join us?" Jane requested.

"If it is to take him to task for causing you such pain, I will make it my life's mission to bring him forthwith!" she winked at her daughter-in-law and whirled out to find her son. "Ha, he got off easy. When I was birthing my first, I demanded that my chamber door be barred against my husband," Hattie nodded when Jane laughed.

As Lady Rose left the chambers to inform her first her son, and then the new grandfather and the collection of new aunts and uncles, Madeline Gardiner took the young Marquess, who was sated, and Tammy passed her daughter the new little Lady.

As his mother opened the library door, Perry looked at her with both trepidation and hope. "Go to your wife, my son; all is well." The words were hardly out of her mouth when Perry jumped out of his chair and sprinted towards the stairs. "Thomas, you are the grandfather of two very healthy babes, a boy and a girl," Lady Rose informed the new grandfather.

"And Jane is well?" he asked, needing to know that more than that, the babes were well. Jane was his first born and would always be the one who opened his heart to the depths of love a parent can have for a child.

"She is, and she did very well. She did not even curse at Perry too much during her labours," Lady Rose smiled.

"I rather wish she was less serene; I would have loved to hear what she might have said. I believe my Tammy threatened to close up my book room when she was birthing the twins." He chuckled.

"Uncle John sounds very well," John Manning used his new title for the first time.

"Yes," Bennet confirmed, "you boys are all uncles now, and Kitty, you are an Aunt."

Her mission complete, Lady Rose returned to the birthing chambers and walked in to see her son looking completely besotted as he gazed on his son's face.

"You did so well, my beloved Jane," he stated, his emotions choking him as he stroked his son's head and then his daughters in turn.

"What will we name them, Perry?" Jane asked, smiling beatifically as she looked up at him, a much more relaxed look than when she was cursing her husband for the pain of childbirth.

"If it meets your approval, I think that Sedgewick Thomas sounds good for our son," Perry suggested as he looked at the tightly swaddled and sleeping form in his arms.

"That is perfect for him, and we can call him Sed," Jane approved. "For our daughter, how does Elizabeth Marie Rose sound? We can call her Beth, so there is never any confusion with her namesake?" Jane looked down at her sleeping daughter in her arms.

"I could not have conceived of a better name for her, my love," Perry agreed, bursting with parental pride. "I would like to take Sed and Beth down to meet their grandpapa, aunt, and uncles." Jane nodded and handed Beth to Aunt Maddie.

When Perry entered the library and introduced the twins to their grandpapa, great uncles, aunt, and uncles, Bennet choked up when he heard that his granddaughter, who was sleeping peacefully in his arms, was named after her aunt Elizabeth.

Before the sun set on the day, news that the Duchess had delivered an heir and a daughter spread through the estate, Bedford, and the surrounding area like wildfire, resulting in much celebrating now that continuity of the Bedford line was assured.

~~~~~~~/~~~~~~~

The carriage bearing the newlywed Darcys arrived at the Golden Cock Inn as dusk descended on the land. They were welcomed with much deference by the landlord, who was making a tidy sum by keeping a whole floor reserved. He showed the couple to their suite himself and then bowed and left them, noticing both Biggs and Johns taking up station in the hall.

Will lifted his bride in his arms and carried her into the suite, kicking the door shut behind them. "Finally alone," Will growled.

"Ahem," Carstens cleared his throat. Will had forgotten that his valet and his wife's lady's maid had travelled ahead with their trunks. "Miss Thénardier and I have baths ready for you if you would like to bathe and change," he informed the couple, keeping his head bowed so he would hide his amusement.

"A bath would be very welcome, husband," Elizabeth allowed, and he set her on her feet. "Mayhap, we can have some food ready for us when we are changed?"

"I agree, Lizzy," Will conceded. Though eager to pick up where they left off in the carriage, washing and eating now would make for fewer interruptions later.

Within an hour later, they met in the sitting room where their repast awaited them. He was wearing a banyan over his nightshirt and breeches while Elizabeth was wearing a robe of light green over what looked like a yellow nightgown. The two dismissed their personal servants for the night, requesting that they not be disturbed until they rang for them in the morning.

Both picked at their meals, but after less than fifteen minutes, and by mutual non-verbal agreement, they rose, and Will led his bride into his bed-chamber. As soon as he closed the door, they fell into one another's arms. Their kisses proved they hungered, but it was not for the abandoned meal. Elizabeth pulled away, but before Will could misunderstand why she opened the robe, and it fell off her shoulders to pool at her feet.

Will gasped at the beauty arrayed before him; the yellow nightgown was as sheer as could be and left nothing to the imagination. His eyes dipped from her face to her fulsome breasts with the dark pink pert nipples, then traversed lower until he spied the triangle of dark hair that promised the secrets he had long coveted. Just seeing her before him as he had dreamed of so many times almost took him beyond his control, but he willed himself to wait.

"You are wearing far too much clothing for the occasion," Elizabeth said saucily as she arched her eyebrow. In the blink of an eye, the banyan was on the floor, followed by his nightshirt. Elizabeth raked her eyes over his handsome face, her eyes entranced with the sight of his well-defined chest, which had some downy hair that tapered and disappeared beneath his breeches. "I want to see *all* of my husband," Elizabeth demanded as she stepped forward and lifted the sheer nightgown over her head, the challenge and expectation making him grin.

Elizabeth gasped when she saw his swollen manhood once he opened and stepped out of his breeches. Neither moved as they drank in the wonders of the sight before them. When she started to reach for him, she broke his trance, and he swept Elizabeth up in his arms and laid her on top of the coverlet on the enormous bed. He laid down next to her, his hands sliding from her neck to her breasts, reminding her of the pleasure of his touch when his fingers brushed her nipples, causing his wife to moan in pleasure, and she again arched her back as she ached for more of his touch.

He lowered his mouth onto one breast and first flicked the tip, and when she mewled, he swirled his tongue around it, making it as hard and swollen, then turned his attention to the other and repeating the process just as thoroughly until he was sure she was as needy as he. When her hand started to travel his body in a bid for more, he slowly slid a hand down her stomach, and he was surprised when she opened her thighs for him, impatient for him to continue rather than show fright or reluctance.

At the touch of his fingers, a flood of promise soaked them, and he proved his appreciation by teasing her open in search of her nub and started to rub it. Elizabeth then shocked him by resting her fingers over his and guided him, showing him what she liked most and when he took over, she moved with his hand to take what she needed, which made him moan in need. When he slipped in one finger, she gasped in surprise, and his tension skyrocketed as he readied her for him.

She reciprocated, sliding her hand down his length.

"This is what I did when I imagined this moment with you." He guided her hand as she had his, helping her learn his desires quicker. For him, the world ceased when she rested her hand over his to cease his ministrations.

"Make me your wife in every way, Will," she demanded.

"Your wish is my command!" He settled over her. She felt the head of his appendage against her core, and then the sensations intensified as he entered her slowly. While all of that had been pleasurable before, it was nothing to this.

He reached the barrier of her maidenhood and stopped, knowing that he was about to cause her pain. Rather than allow him to worry, she thrust her hips toward him, and in the same instant, he tore through the final vestige of her being a maiden he was fully seated in her. She gasped, pausing his words by resting a hand over his heart, and gave them both the comfort of eye contact. In this deeper connection they had, she comforted him as the pain was expected and a relief for her because that meant she was his wife in all ways at long last.

"Make love with me, Will." She asked softly. At first, he moved slowly, but this first time with her was overwhelming and too soon over as he could not help but lose himself in his Lizzy, and in understanding that he would not last long, stroked her as she had taught him and took them over the edge together.

He rolled off her, and they finally got under the covers. "You are not further in pain, are you, Lizzy?" Will asked with concern.

"There was but a moment, and it passed, and what little there is now expected when one is using their body in a new way. It is better than anything I imagined when I would daydream of what it would be like to become your wife at last," she owned without embarrassment.

"You used to think of me, together with you? I love that you are no simpering miss, and I can express my passion without fear of overwhelming you, Lizzy. Tell me you only thought of me as you pleasured yourself." He asked as his fingers again started to stroke her again.

"Only you!" she promised as she slid her fingers up his length. His mouth took hers, and he lifted her over him, her surprise making him grin.

"You feel deeper," she whispered in awe.

"Make love to me, Lizzy!" he begged.

"Your wish is my command." She replied, her tone sultry and full of promise as she moved in the ways his hands guided her until she figured out exactly what was possible, and all sense of time was lost in the pleasure one can only experience when they are with someone they love completely.

CHAPTER 16

"Will you not tell me where you are taking me for our wedding trip, husband? We are about to board Perry's ship in Southampton. Please tell me where we are going, Will," Elizabeth beseeched her husband, her excitement his undoing.

"I suppose it will do no harm now that you know we are to sail to a destination. We are going to the Kingdom of Sicily and the Papal States on the Italian peninsular, my love," Will informed his bride.

"Thank you, thank you, thank you, Will!" she looked up at him in perfect joy. "I have wanted to travel to some of the lands that you described while on your Grand Tour for the longest time so that I could see the same sights you did. You could not have planned a better trip for me if you had tried!"

The Darcys were shown to the owner's cabin, a most spacious area that abutted the ship's stern. It encompassed the entire width from port to starboard and was more than one-third of the vessel's length. There was a cavernous dining/sitting room area, a large cabin with a bed not much smaller than the one at Rivington, and two small cabins for the personal servants.

"I cannot wait to make love to my wife as we sail towards our destination," Will growled in Elizabeth's ear, sending chills down her spine.

"Unlike Oxford, hopefully, we actually get to see some of the sights in the countries we are to visit and not just the inside of our chambers," Elizabeth teased him.

"I would desire to never leave our chambers, but we will see as many of the sights that you wish, my love." Will silenced her reply with a kiss that made her knees weaken, then stepped back, looking quite pleased with himself. "Mayhap, you want to put yourself to rights so we may stand on deck and watch the sights as we sail."

"As it was you that caused the state I am in, you smug man, you are tasked with assisting me!" Elizabeth replied pertly.

A few minutes later, the newlyweds found a spot on the port side next to the railing where they watched as the men on the quay slipped the ships lines, then the jib and two smaller sails were raised, and they caught the seaward wind which pulled the ship from the quay. Once clear of the dock, Will and Elizabeth watched as the crew climbed up the rigging as surely as one would walk on solid ground and released the mainsail, which billowed as it caught the wind. The vessel started to gain some speed as she pointed toward the open sea and their destination beyond.

July 29, 1799

Elizabeth rested against the solid chest of her husband as the ship sailed up the Thames towards the dock where they would finally disembark, and then the wedding trip that would forever be an extremely happy memory for both would be over. Will had kept his word; they had explored and seen as many sights as Elizabeth desired.

Elizabeth had loved exploring Rome and all the churches of the Papal States. She had found St. Peter's Basilica fascinating and loved exploring the catacombs below the city. The highlight was seeing the Sistine Chapel and marvelling at the work of Michelangelo on the magnificently painted ceiling.

The ship was tied up to the dock, and they smiled when they saw the Darcy carriage waiting for them on the street above the dock. It was less than five hours to Broadhurst in Essex, where their family was currently staying. With Biggs and Johns carrying most of their trunks between them, the Darcys were soon ready to set foot on England's soil after almost six weeks of traveling abroad. Before disembarking, they thanked the captain profusely then made their way to the quay.

Both laughed at the feeling that the ground was moving under their feet, for when they had reached Licata on the Island of Sicily after six days at sea and felt the sensation for the first time, both had been concerned until the smiling captain, who had accompanied them ashore, explained that it was a natural occurrence when one who had been on a ship for any length of time walked on dry land again.

~~~~~~~/~~~~~~~

When the conveyance halted at Broadhurst, Elizabeth and Will had barely alighted when the family mobbed them with Georgiana leading the charge.

"Were you surprised, Lizzy?" Georgiana gushed after she hugged both her brother and sister.

"I was, Gigi. It was the best of surprises," Elizabeth told her sister.

"How well you look, Lizzy," her mother said as she enfolded her daughter in a hug. "It seems that married life agrees with you." By the blush that her daughter answered with, Lady Elaine did not doubt the veracity of her supposition.

"Welcome home, sister and brother," Alex said as he shook his brother's hand and kissed his new sister's hand as a young gentleman might; then the boy re-emerged, "Did you bring many gifts home?" he asked hopefully.

"We did, little brother. Mayhap you will allow us to change and wash before you demand your presents?" Will said as he ruffled his brother's hair, who scowled back as he tried to flatten it back into place.

Next, they were hugged by Lady Anne and George Darcy. "Welcome back to England, Son, and Daughter," Lady Anne kissed both on their cheeks while her husband hugged his son and bestowed a kiss on his new daughter.

"This dullard is treating you well, is he not?" Richard drawled as he looked at his brother-in-law.

"Itch! I mean Richard, Will could not treat me better if he tried. And you, brother? How are you and Retta with only three days to go before you join the blissful state Will and I now inhabit?"

"We are both excited, Lizzy," Loretta said as she gave her betrothed a warning look that it was enough teasing—for now. "I am so pleased that your arrival was not delayed, and you are here to be with us for our wedding day."

"As we are happy to be here, my soon-to-be sister," Elizabeth promised. "Andrew and Marie! I almost did not see you hiding there. My, how much bigger little Reggie is, and Tiffany also. We were away for less than two months, and my niece and nephew… oh, I am so ashamed I did not ask sooner; did Jane she deliver her babe safely?"

"She did, Lizzy," Marie informed her sister. "But it was babies, not babe, and Jane, their son, and their daughter are all well and healthy. They will arrive on the morrow with the Bennets, who have been at Longfield Meadows since little Sed and Beth made their entry into the world, on the day of your wedding by the by."

"The day of our wedding and Beth?" Elizabeth asked in wonder.

"Elizabeth Marie Rose Rhys-Davies," Andrew added. "For some reason, Jane wanted to name her daughter after you. Jane sent an express to the inn near Bedford; I assume that by your questions, you did not receive it."

"We did not," Will confirmed.

"Mayhap, it is time to allow Will and Lizzy to repair to their chambers," Lady Sarah De Melville suggested. "They will be here until after the wedding, so there will be ample time to see them."

"Is Bingley coming?" Will asked Richard as they made their way into the manor house.

"Unfortunately, his wife has been having a tough time with illness associated with increasing, so he will remain at Netherfield as being in a carriage exacerbates her symptoms," Richard explained.

"Let us hope that all will be well for young Mrs. Bingley and the babe that she is carrying," Will replied.

~~~~~~~/~~~~~~~

The Bennets and Rhys-Davies arrived before midday the next

SHANA GRANDERSON A LADY

day. Elizabeth could not wait to hug Jane and see her niece and nephew as they entered the drawing room. After the sisters hugged for a long while, Jane turned to a nursemaid holding a squirming bundle and handed little Beth to the aunt after whom she was named.

"She is perfect, Jane. She has your blond hair and eyes and so much hair!" Elizabeth exclaimed. "We never received your express; I am so sorry I would have loved to have known before we sailed."

"She seems to have claimed all the hair that was available for the both of them," the proud papa joked as he held his son close by but allowing the sisters to reconnect and take a moment with his daughter. If she were even half as amazing as her mother and aunt, she would be a force to be reckoned with indeed. "As you can see, Sed is still bald."

"He has Jane's eyes as well!" Elizabeth gushed as she held her niece.

"Do not forget, Lizzy, that a babe's eyes can change up to the age of six months, so we will not know the true colours until they pass that milestone in a little more than four months," Lady Rose said.

"Father Bennet and Mother Tammy, it is good to see you again," Will welcomed them while his wife was lost in the world of babies.

"When did you inform my daughter where you were taking her for the wedding trip?" Bennet grinned.

"The day we sailed from Southampton," Will shared.

Elizabeth did not relinquish her niece until she placed her into the waiting cradle in the nursery. "How did they do on their first carriage ride, Jane?" Elizabeth asked as she walked with Jane to show her which suite was hers and Perry's.

"They did surprisingly well; I believe it was the way that Perry planned the trip. We stopped often and did not travel as far as we could have each day. Rather than two, the trip was four days. My husband is a doting and most considerate father," Jane informed her younger sister. "Now tell me, how did you enjoy your honeymoon, sister dearest?"

"It could not have been better, Will chose the perfect thing as he knew how much I wanted to travel," Elizabeth told Jane.

"And how is the, well, the rest of your marriage?" Jane asked as delicately as she could.

"With nothing to compare to, I would still say that the personal part of our union is as good as it could be," said the blushing bride. "Luckily, my mother and Mother Tammy let me know that desiring my husband did not make me a wanton and was, in fact, perfectly natural and right."

"Mama told me the same before I married my Perry," Jane agreed. "I can hardly believe that we are in our third year of marriage; time goes by like the blink of an eye."

"That is why we need to enjoy each day that God allows us in this world!" Elizabeth hugged her older sister and went in search of her husband to see if he wanted to join her for a 'rest,' which she very much hoped he too wanted.

~~~~~~~~/~~~~~~~~

The night before the wedding, Richard was with the men in one of the drawing rooms, being ribbed mercilessly by his newest brother. "Peace Will, you have returned the favour from before your wedding tenfold!" Richard exclaimed good-naturedly.

"That I have," Will returned with a smug look. "Did I not promise you that I would have my day?"

"If I am able to attain half of the felicity that I see between you and Lizzy, we will be very happy," Richard stated as he changed the subject.

"That is my wish for you and my sister," Wes stated and then took another sip from the snifter of brandy in his hand. "There is no need to admonish you to treat her well as I have no doubt that you will. I look forward to gaining a slew of brothers and sisters on the morrow."

"You two are far too besotted, one with the other not to have a felicitous marriage," Andrew opined as he held up his snifter in salute to his brother.

"Is everything organised at Lake View House for your arrival,

Richard?" Will asked.

"Yes, thanks to Andrew, all is organised. Uncle George and Aunt Anne offered Seaview as well. If Loretta wants to extend the trip, then we will spend a few weeks there after the Lakes," Richard replied.

The men did not stay up too late as the wedding was at nine in the morning, and Richard would have their heads if they made him late for it.

~~~~~~~/~~~~~~~

Loretta had just received the talk from her mother. Like Lizzy and Jane before her, what her mother imparted washed her anxiety away and made her long for the wedding night. As Lizzy's wedding night was, hers would be at an inn, but Loretta cared not so long as she was able to be with her Richard.

After her mother left her chambers, she was joined by Elizabeth and Jane. "It sounds like your mother's talk was very similar to the one we received from our mothers before our wedding," Jane told the bride after Retta related its gist.

"Yes, and I can tell you that it is very good advice, especially the part about not being afraid to ask what gives your husband pleasure or telling him what is pleasurable to you," Elizabeth informed her soon-to-be sister. "Even showing him. Apparently, men are more visual, so my husband promised they very much liked that."

"Did…I mean…was there much pain and blood the first time?" Loretta asked softly that her only fear remaining.

"There was some momentary pain but nothing significant, and each time we repeated the exercise, it became less," Elizabeth explained. "There was little blood in my case."

"Richard will not want to cause you pain, so if it hurts more than you can easily manage as it did with me, then I am sure that he will wait until you are ready to proceed," Jane offered the wisdom of her perspective. "For me, there was a bit more blood than Lizzy described, but remember that it is different for every woman."

"I thank you both. While Mama eased the anxiety, I find the

recounting of your experiences tremendously helpful," Loretta said.

The three chatted for another hour when Jane had to leave to feed her babes.

"In the morning, we will be sisters, Lizzy," Loretta stated. "I love your brother most dearly."

"And he is deeply in love with you, Retta," Elizabeth told her soon-to-be sister. "Sleep well, and before you know it, you will be at the altar as the parson pronounces you man and wife.

~~~~~~~/~~~~~~~

"The Honourable Mr. Richard Fitzwilliam and Lady Loretta Fitzwilliam," Broadhurst's butler intoned proudly as the newly-weds entered the ballroom to cheers from the assembled guests. Loretta was glowing, and Richard was grinning from ear to ear.

They made the rounds to greet guests, and Elizabeth and Will returned the courtesy from their own wedding by taking Loretta and Richard to sit for a while so that they might partake of their own wedding breakfast. The break was very welcome as the bride and groom were off their feet for the first time in a few hours as Broadhurst's church was walking distance from the house.

After both Lords Cyril and Wes made toasts to the happy couple, it was time to change into their travelling attire. Lady Sarah accompanied her daughter to the chambers, which had been Loretta's since she had left the nursery. "You look like a very happy woman, Loretta," her mother told her as she was assisted out of her wedding gown by a maid as her lady's maid and Richard's valet were already on the way to the first inn.

"I am, Mama. Richard and I are perfectly balanced, and I could never imagine loving any life partner any more than I do him," Loretta stated as she stepped into her travel gown.

"It will be hard not to see you every day, Loretta," Lady Sarah said, "so I will look forward to seeing you during the upcoming little season."

"A girl could not have wished for a better mother, Mama. I will miss you too, but it is the way of our world, is it not? We marry and then cleave ourselves unto our husbands and leave our father's homes," Loretta stated.

Mother and daughter shared a tearful hug then descended the stairs arm in arm where Richard was waiting for his new wife.

The De Melville's, Fitzwilliams, Darcys, and Ryes-Davies accompanied them to the waiting carriage under the portico. "Look after my baby," Lord Cyril told his new son.

"You know that I will do so always and to the best of my abilities, Father Cyril," Richard replied firmly.

"We just returned, and now I must farewell you again, Rich," Elizabeth hugged her brother tightly.

"Have an enjoyable wedding trip, Richard, and we will see you when you return to Brookfield," his mother said as she hugged her younger son. "All my children are wed now, so I will just have to wait for my grandchildren's weddings!"

The family stood back and waved as the driver put the team into motion. Once the carriage took the turn towards the estate's gate, the family returned inside to be with the wedding guests.

CHAPTER 17

The Fitzwilliams arrived at the Roaring Lion Inn just before sunset. The sky was a pallet of oranges, reds, and golds as the sun dipped below the horizon on their wedding day. Richard had reserved the largest suite of rooms that the landlord had. The couple were pleased with what they found. Their personal servants were waiting for them, so in short, the order had baths drawn for their master and mistress.

Without having to say the words, both agreed that they would eat in their suite and had no interest utilising the private parlour offered for their use. Richard, who normally wolfed down any food in his general vicinity, only ate half of his food while his wife pecked at hers.

"Are you well, Loretta?" Richard asked out of concern.

"I find I am a little too warm, husband," Loretta replied with a saucy look.

"Let me lower the fire," Richard stood as he had not caught her intent yet.

"Richard," she called softly.

He turned around and froze at the spectacular sight before him. His wife was naked with her robe and nightgown strewn on the floor.

"I see I misunderstood when you said you were warm," Richard said as he approached his wife, licking his lips as he prepared to kiss her in full appreciation of her gift.

"You are far too overdressed for the occasion, Richard; I want to see all of you, too," Loretta stated breathily. It was, but an instant before Richard's nightshirt was flung away—where, he cared not.

It was Loretta's turn to allow her eyes to roam over her husband's form. He had broad shoulders, a well-defined barrel chest, and muscular belly. His chest sported a covering of almost blond hair that tapered downward.

They came together, and Richard pulled her into him. Richard picked Loretta up as if she weighed naught, carrying her into the bed chamber, and lowered her on top of himself on the bed.

Though he was a man of the world, she was far more forward with him than he had dared hope, and a woman who could take what she needed from him was a possibility he had not dared hope for until they were years in.

Just before Loretta was about to take her release, Richard lowered her to her back. He walked to the end of the bed and then lay down between her legs. "Do you trust me, dearest?" he asked, his eyes twinkling in the candlelight.

"With all that I am," She replied, her breath heavy with anticipation. Grateful she was no wilting flower, he devoured her, taking her past her release into an endless ecstasy that had her so blissful she could not but smile dreamily up at him when he settled over her. "Love me with all of you, Richard." She asked softly, barely registering the pain when he slid in as pleasure returned in delicious waves that made her whole body quiver.

"I believe we will have a marriage most would not dare dream of." He chuckled.

"Only if you stop being so slow to come to the point." She smiled up at him in a playful challenge few would appreciate more than a soldier who worried he would be too much for his gentle wife.

"My apologies." He kissed her soundly then proceeded to make love to his wife until the sunrise proved time had not stopped.

~~~~~~~/~~~~~~~

Two days after the wedding, the Darcys arrived at Pemberley. For Will and Elizabeth, it was a most welcome sight having by then almost two months away from Derbyshire. The couple would stay at Pemberley overnight and then depart for Rivington in the morning. It was close enough that they could have easily made the estate before sundown, but they had been invited to spend the night with their family.

After dinner, all six Darcys and William Bennet were sitting in the music room where Georgiana had just completed a duet with her mother.

"How are you finding your duties, William?" Elizabeth asked her older brother.

"I am finding that I enjoy them very well," William replied. "There is much to learn, and Mr. Perkins is a good teacher. Thankfully, he is the type of clergyman that I want to be, like Mr. Price at Longbourn is. He does not see his livings as a means of income, but rather a calling, and the welfare of every single parishioner, regardless of rank, is important to him."

"He is a good man, William," George Darcy agreed, "and he finds that you are too. He is to retire at the end of November and has heartily endorsed my choice to appoint you to his livings."

"Are you sure, Uncle George, for I am yet young?" William reminded him.

"I have had your measure for a long time, William, including long conversations with Mr. Pierce, who told me how you would take the shirt off your back to help someone if you thought it was warranted. It is not age but temperament that I look for in my appointments, and you have exactly what I am looking for to guide the parishioners of the three parishes I can grant a living for."

"Look at how well you performed our wedding ceremony barely a month after you had taken orders, William. With your legacy, you could be an indolent gentleman and live well, but you choose to follow the call of God and His Son Jesus," Elizabeth said with pride in her brother.

"In that case, I thank you, Uncle George. I will not let you down." He nodded to the room at large. No one noted that Georgiana seemed to look pleased when it was confirmed that William Bennet would remain in the area, except her mother, who could not but smile at the possibility of such a perfect match for her daughter. Thomas Bennet had indeed been a patriarch of good fortune for their family. Perhaps a first edition from the top shelves would be an appropriate gift for him.

"Lizzy and Will, may I come with you to Rivington on the morrow?" Georgiana asked, pleading sweetly with wide, innocent eyes.

"Me too," Alex added.

"Before your brother or sister answer, let me stop you two there," their father stated firmly. "It will be the first day that Lizzy and Will are at their estate as a married couple." He gave his two younger children a quelling look before they spoke again. "When they are settled in, and they *invite* you, then you may go with pleasure."

"Father George is correct. In a...," Elizabeth looked to her husband.

"Week," Will suggested the timelines they had already discussed before inviting them.

"Yes, you are all welcome in a week. I am issuing my first official invitation as Mistress of Rivington," Elizabeth effused. "I will send an invitation to Mama, Marie, and Andrew as well. It is a pity that Jane and Perry will be at Longbourn until the little season."

"If my parents will cede this Christmastide to us, why do we not have all of the family at Rivington for the holiday?" Will suggested, looking at his parents to gauge their reaction.

"I see no reason why you and Lizzy should not host your first Christmastide," Lady Anne said after her husband nodded. "Both your mother and I will be available to assist you as needed, Lizzy."

"Marie will also want to help. She has hosted the holiday more than once since she became the mistress of Snowhaven," Elizabeth added as she started making plans in her mind. "Now that Retta is my sister, Aunt Sarah and Uncle Cyril will have to be included at all family events."

"I, for one, am happy that Wes is your brother and no more than that!" Will teased his wife.

"He never stood a chance, Will. I had lost my heart to an

infuriating man, and in the end, none but him would do," Elizabeth said with an arched eyebrow at her grinning husband.

~~~~~~~/~~~~~~~

Will and Elizabeth now had a suite that would always be ready for them at Pemberley. It was a few doors down from the master suite, which both prayed would not be theirs for many years. "Are you ready to be loved, my Lizzy?" Will asked as he climbed into the bed next to his wife.

"Nothing would please me more, but I am indisposed my love," Elizabeth told her husband delicately.

"Well then, I see we will have to be a bit more inventive," Will said with a glint in his eye.

"There is nothing to stop me pleasuring you," Elizabeth said as she slid her hand up his thigh.

~~~~~~~/~~~~~~~

The Darcys arrived at Rivington before midday. The butler, housekeeper, and servants were arrayed to meet them, and they accepted congratulations on their nuptials from all assembled. "My husband and I are happy to return home. We will rely on each of you to make Rivington the best that it can be. I hope to learn all your names in a short time, and though we demand respect, we believe in giving respect in return. Thank you for your warm welcome and well wishes."

The butler and housekeeper dismissed the servants, who all left the entrance hall feeling that they would enjoy working for the young master and mistress. "Mrs. Ralston, please inform Cook that we will have dinner at half after six in the breakfast parlour. When it is just the two of us, there is no need to bother with the formal dining room," Elizabeth instructed before she and her husband ascended the stairs.

They noted that the few changes they had requested in their sitting room had been done to precision, as was the mistress's chambers. The master's bed would be the one that they would use, and the only time they planned to use Elizabeth's bed was when she was in her final confinement if they were so blessed. Thankfully, there was no pressure on them to produce an heir. If they had all daughters, or worse yet no children, Alex's, or, failing that, Georgiana's son, would inherit Pemberley after Will.

"Welcome home, Mrs. Darcy," Will said as he started to dance an impromptu waltz with his wife. Even though London society rejected the dance as scandalous, as Will had promised, he had taught Elizabeth the dance on the continent, and they joined it as many times as they could before returning to England.

"When do you think this dance will be accepted in London?" Elizabeth asked as they twirled around the chamber.

"We do have a remarkably close connection to one of Almack's patronesses, Lizzy. Mayhap we can work on Aunt Sarah. I believe that until the dance starts being acceptable at private balls, it will not be allowed in wider society," Will opined.

"We may have to start holding balls in London," Elizabeth teased.

~~~~~~~/~~~~~~~

End of September 1799

In the end, Richard and Loretta decided to forego time at Seaview Cottage. Both Darcy's families and William Bennet were visiting Snowhaven when Richard's barouche came to a halt in the drive.

Richard told Smythe not to announce him and his wife, so the family was caught by complete surprise when the happy couple strode into the drawing room. "Richard and Loretta, welcome," Marie was the first to react. "We were not aware that you would be here today; you are most welcome as always."

"I decided I was tired of being alone with Richard, so we returned home," Loretta teased her mockingly aggrieved husbands, who then leaned for her to kiss his cheek in recompense and grinned at the winning of it.

"It has been much warmer than normal, so we decided not to travel for four days in this heat," Richard clarified.

"That was a wise decision," George Darcy agreed, "I do not remember heat like this so late in the summer for many a year."

"How was your time at Lakeview House?" Elizabeth enquired.

"We, er, did not see as much of the area as we could have." Richard owned, pleased his wife smiled at him instead of shrinking away in embarrassment.

"When are you two planning to head to Brookfield?" Andrew asked.

"When do you depart for Rivington, Lizzy?" Loretta inquired.

"We are planning to leave Monday," Will replied.

Richard looked at Loretta, and she nodded to his unspoken question. "Then we will leave on Monday too, if that is convenient, Marie?"

"Of course it is," Marie replied, "and besides, you are always welcome in this house with or without notice. Glad you agree." She patted her husband's knee absently.

Elaine Fitzwilliam sat watching the happy scene in front of her. It was times like this that she especially felt the loss of her beloved Reggie, though she was sure that he was smiling down on them from heaven.

She wondered how different their lives would have been had her boys not been traveling through Sherwood Forest at exactly the right time, for Lizzy had brought so much light and joy into their lives since that very day. She had survived multiple attempts to harm her and gone from strength to strength, and now she was married to her soulmate.

Yes, Elaine had lost her Reggie and would miss him until she was called home by God to be with her love again, but there was so much good associated with Lizzy though there had been suffering and heartache. They had been shells of their former selves after the accident which had taken their Tiffany from them, and they had all started to recover the day Lizzy had been gifted to their family.

Elaine could not imagine what their lives would have been like without Lizzy having been someone's discarded daughter.

EPILOGUE

The master and mistress of Pemberley were seated on the veranda overlooking the gardens and a grassy area near the treeline where several children were playing with their two Great Danes who had been acquired from the same breeder as the late great Aggie. After twelve years of marriage, Elizabeth and Will were more in love now than they had ever been.

Much had changed in the country and the world. The Little Tyrant had declared himself Emperor of France and had started a war in May 1803 to gain countries for his Empire. In England, the Prince of Wales was made Regent as of the current year. An attempt to declare a regency had been thwarted some years previously, but there was no denying any longer how sick the King was, and those who blocked passage of the establishment of a regency before had not done so this time.

Elizabeth had warm memories of old King George III from the times that she had exhibited for the monarchs in her younger days. It was sad, but there were few who denied the necessity of the step declaring the King unfit to govern.

Not everything had been smooth sailing. There had been the deep sadness of George Darcy's passing when he had fallen from a horse as he was jumping a fence during the hunt some three years earlier.

The doctor had opined that death had been instantaneous; George Darcy's neck had been snapped on contact with the ground. Pegasus, his horse, had two broken legs, and the screaming animal had been shot to put him out of his misery.

As could be expected, Lady Anne had been devastated at losing her soul mate and had only recently gone into half-mourning. As Elizabeth was with child for the third time, Will had foregone the hunt and stayed with his very pregnant wife.

A week after the death of their father and father-in-law respectively, Will and Elizabeth moved to Pemberley, though they were sorry to leave Rivington as they had been extremely happy at the estate. It was decided that when Ben married, he would be gifted Rivington, as Will had been when he married his beloved Elizabeth.

Anne Darcy had wanted to move to the dower house, and Elizabeth and Will wanted her to remain in the mistress' suite, so a compromise was enacted. The grieving widow would move into the suite that her son and daughter-in-law had until then used, which was then designated as the Dower Suite.

The hardest thing for Will was sitting behind his father's desk in the master's study. As much as he missed his father, he knew that he had to carry on as the last thing that George Darcy would have wanted was for Pemberley and all who depended on the estate to suffer because of his death. Luckily, the steward was exceptionally good at his job, and he had assisted the new master as needed until Will had felt comfortable with all his tasks. His father had trained him and trained him well, but it was hard to take the reins fully for the first few months in his grief.

There had been the stillborn child between the first and third child born to Elizabeth and Will. The cord had somehow become wrapped around the babe's neck that had resulted in her death. The result of the birth had sent Elizabeth spiralling into a depression that her husband and family had been concerned she would not survive. Bringing Ben—Bennet George, their firstborn —who had been born the tenth of November 1800, a year to the day after the *coup d'état* that brought Napoleon Bonaparte to power in France, to his ailing wife. Having the almost two-year-old try to play with his Mama had somehow reached her when all else had failed.

Thankfully, Ben had pierced the veneer of her depression, and

Elizabeth had started to recover. Once she was well again, she shared that she had blamed herself for her daughter's death but finally accepted that it was not so. Their second son, George, was born two years after Elizabeth's recovery, and the long-awaited daughter, Priscilla Beth, named for her late great-grandmothers, was born two months after the tragic death of her grandfather George.

Two other deaths had saddened them all. The first was Anne Ashby. After several years, Anne had conceived, and everything had looked good until the midwife had attempted to deliver the babe, a girl, who was breech. The babe did not live more than a few minutes, and her mother joined her daughter with God soon after, as neither the doctor nor the midwife could stem the haemorrhaging.

A devastated Ian did not want Rosings without his late wife as he still had Sherwood Park in Surrey, so he relinquished it to Richard and Loretta's second son Andy. Her death had hit her Mother, Elaine, and family extremely hard as she had been so long their daughter and sister that she was mourned as much as any sibling and child might be.

The second death was Lady Rose Ryes-Davies' a year after the loss of Will's father. She had contracted flu, and the fever kept increasing until it took her after a battle of three days. Jane and Perry, and Marie and Andrew, not to mention the rest of the family, had felt her loss very keenly.

Two years after the twins, Jane had given birth to a daughter, Tammy Rose, followed almost three years later by Lydia Jane. Less than two years later, the last of Jane and Perry's children, Maxwell, to be called Max, was born. Due to complications with the delivery of the afterbirth, Jane was unable to deliver another child. They were sad that there would be no more but were grateful for the five healthy children they had, even more so that all five had been born before Lady Rose was lost.

Three years after Tiffany was born, Andrew and Marie welcomed Richard William to their family, and two years after him, Penelope Rose became the fourth child and second daughter to be gifted to the Earl and Countess of Matlock.

Loretta and Richard rivalled Elizabeth and Will in felicity in their marriage. Less than a year after their wedding, Brookfield's heir was born. Grant Cyril Fitzwilliam was the first of six children—so far. Two daughters, Sarah, barely a year after her brother, and Lucinda, called Lucy, born less than two years later, came next. They were followed by Andrew, called Andy, Jackson, called Jack and Cassandra Anne, called Cassy Anne, spaced out about a year and a half between each.

As much as they mourned Anne, they were not unhappy that their second son Andy would not have to shift for himself. Thankfully, Jack had the gift of the gab, so they envisaged him reading the law one day.

The biggest surprise to most of the family was the betrothal of Georgiana Darcy and William Bennet in April of 1804 when Georgiana had turned twenty. She had two London seasons and had never found anyone vaguely interesting to her. The truth of their romance was unknown to most of the family but was not a rash decision. Evidently, the two had started having tender feelings for one another some years before.

Two and a half years after their wedding, Jane Anne Bennet joined the world. She was named for William's late mother and his father's sister, and her maternal grandmother. Less than two years later, little Tommy George Bennet arrived. Georgiana was currently increasing with her third child.

Even though William's legacy had grown exponentially over the years and with the addition of Georgiana's dowry, they could have easily purchased an estate; they never chose to leave the parsonage at Pemberley, which was the largest of the three rectories in the parishes for which William held the livings.

Of all of Elizabeth's Bennet siblings, only Tom remained unmarried. James had married one of the Goulding daughters in a surprise to all who had thought that he and Georgiana would one day form tender feelings, but if any had bothered to ask either of the principals, they would have been informed that the two saw each other as no more than brother and sister.

Some years ago, Kitty had requested that she be called Catherine, married a man from Bedfordshire who, after their marriage, inherited his family's large estate. They so far had been blessed with a son and two daughters.

John Manning had married the daughter of the head of the firm that he worked for and was a much sought-after barrister in London. They had one daughter, named after his mother, and his wife was increasing again.

Much to Bennet's pleasure, as Kitty was in Staffordshire, he and Tammy spent a minimum of four months a year in the north where Bennet was able to visit the various libraries on his relatives' estates, though he would always make sure that he had the most time in Pemberley's library. He felt the loss of one of his best friends when George Darcy's accident robbed the family of his presence.

Bennet and Tammy had many grandchildren and cherished every single one of them. The Darcy children had never questioned why they were so lucky as to have three grandmamas; they just accepted it as fact and enjoyed being spoiled during a visit from any or all of them together.

A year earlier, Alexander Darcy, who no longer wanted to be called Alex, had married Lady Candace Woolridge, the daughter of the Earl of Oakmont. Will had changed his mind about Rivington with Elizabeth's hearty agreement, and it had been presented to Alexander and Candace as a wedding gift. The two were extremely pleased as they had planned to use his legacy to purchase a smaller estate. Will was certain, and his mother agreed wholeheartedly, that his late father would have agreed with his decision.

When Ben reached that point, there was always Castledale in Yorkshire until he took over Pemberley. The estate was a little smaller than Rivington and cleared between five and six thousand pounds per annum, and like Snowhaven, only the outer wall of the castle remained with the interior having being redecorated by Elizabeth and Lady Anne in the year before the horrific accident.

Now at the ripe old age of thirty, Elizabeth was increasing for the fifth time and praying that this would be a live birth. Unlike her second time increasing, this babe was very active and had been since the quickening. "When do the Hursts and the contingent from Hertfordshire arrive, my love?" Elizabeth asked as she rested her hands on her swollen belly.

"On the morrow, my heart," Will replied, "and the Gardiners and their children. I understand that Lily's betrothed will be part of the party."

After her daughter Mary, Louisa Hurst had only delivered one more babe, another daughter who they had named Caroline in honour of a sister she once had loved and with the hope that she would be nothing like her late aunt.

As expected, Graham Phillips had married Cara Long a little after her eighteenth birthday, and they so far had one child. Franny was married to her father's clerk, who would take over the practice one day. Bingley and Mandy had three boys, Oscar, Charlie, and John. Mandy was with child and praying that she would have a daughter this time.

Martha Bingley accompanied the Hertfordshire party riding with the Long and Phillips parents; her mother had gone to her final reward some six years previously. As much as Martha missed her mother, she was grateful for the time that she had been granted with her.

"Will," Elizabeth called his attention to herself, "if I had not been discarded, would we have met?"

"My belief is that we were always fated for each other, Lizzy, so I would like to think so. I could not imagine my life without you in it," Will replied.

"We will never know; we may have met and argued and disliked one another. As evil as the plan to discard me was, I have to believe that it was fated so that we could be one as we are now," Elizabeth said as she considered the breadth of her life thus far.

"Regardless of how we arrived at this point, I believe that our love is one for the ages that cannot be extinguished by anyone or anything, even death," Will stated as he took his wife's hands.

"Yes, Will, I believe that you are correct. Regardless of how I got here, I am right where I need to be," Elizabeth said as she lifted her husband's hand as kissed them.

The End...or is it?

Later in 2021, look for a sequel: *'Georgiana Darcy and William Bennet Find Love.'*

COMING SOON

Surviving Thomas Bennet

**Warning: This book contains violence, although not graph-
ically portrayed.**

There are Bennet twins born to James Bennet, his heir, James
Junior and second born Thomas. They boys start out as the
best of friends until Thomas starts to get resentful of his older
brother's status as heir.

The younger Bennet turns to gambling, drink, and carousing.
In order to protect Longbourn, unbeknownst to Thomas, James
Bennet senior places and entail on the estate so none of his son's
creditors are able to make demands against the family estate.

Thomas Bennet was given his legacy of thirty thousand
pounds when he reached his majority. He marries Fanny the
daughter of a local solicitor in Oxford where Thomas is teaching.
He is fired for being drunk at work. He manages to gamble away
all of his legacy while going into serious debt to a dangerous
man.

When James Senior dies, Thomas and Fanny Bennet arrive at
Longbourn demanding their inheritance. The find out there is
no more for them and leave after abusing one an all roundly.

James and his wife Priscilla have a son, Jamie, and daughters
Jane, Elizabeth, and Mary. Thinking he can sell Longbourn if his
brother and son are out of the way, Thomas Bennet murders
them and James' wife by causing a carriage accident.

The story reveals how the three surviving daughters are protected by their friends. Netherfield belongs to the Darcy's second
son, William.

There are many of the characters that are both loved and

hated from the canon in this story, some similar to canon, a good number of them hugely different.

The story will be published in June/July 2021

Later in 2021

Unknown Family Connections – This story will be in two or three volumes, in a single book. It starts with a split in a very prominent family in 1655 and we follow the story from that point forward.

The *Take Charge* series – This series will all be standalone stories where a particular Pride & Prejudice character takes charge and exerts her or his influence. We will see how the tale unfolds because of that particular character taking charge for each of the books. Currently 4 – 6 books are planned for the series.

Made in United States
Orlando, FL
15 May 2024

46894670R00107